TILL HELL

FREEZES OVER

By

Anne Barton

DURANGO PUBLISHING CORP.
TILL HELL FREEZES OVER

Original copyright © 2002 by Anne Barton

Published by:
Durango Publishing Corp.
Suite 204 - 69 Nanaimo Ave. East
Penticton, BC, Canada V2A 1M1
Email: DurangoPublishing@shaw.ca
Web: www.DurangoPublishing.com
Tel: 250-490-3000 Toll free order line: 1-800-545-6321

Library and Archives Canada Cataloguing in Publication

Barton, Anne, 1931-
    Till hell freezes over / Anne Barton.

(Dr. Erica Merrill mystery series)
Originally published: Oakville, Ont. : LTD Books, 2002.
ISBN 978-1-55422-020-5

    I. Title. II. Series: Barton, Anne, 1931- Dr. Erica Merrill mystery series.
PS8553.A7775T47 2007   C813'.6   C2007-903013-0

Cover design by Magpye Productions
Printed and bound in Canada

Also by Anne Barton

A Switch in Time
A Dr. Erica Merrill Mystery

Anne Barton

Photo by IPC

To the memory of my parents,
Bob and Milly Burroughs

Though readers acquainted with North Central Idaho may find the landscape familiar and may recognize the fictional city of Lincoln as Lewiston, Idaho, this story is about fictional people and events in a fictional setting.

The imaginary "Lincoln Clarion" bears no resemblance to the award-winning Lewiston Morning Tribune.

CHAPTER 1

On Sunday morning the winter dawn came belatedly to Black Bear Ridge. Saturday night's snowfall had been heavy but brief; the front that brought it roared on and left the air clear but very cold. The temperature dropped precipitously and sent weather conscious residents to their record books looking for precedents.

Snow crunched under the feet of any creature that dared to venture from its shelter. Exhaled breath hung in clouds in front of nostrils and froze in droplets of ice on hair and whiskers. Vegetation uncovered by pawing hooves of horses, cattle and sheep, was frozen and unpalatable. Water was nowhere to be found, and thirsty creatures were forced to lick the snow. Burrowing animals stayed in their dens and barn cats curled up deep in the hay. In the mountains behind the ridge, where the air was even colder, a tree whose sap had frozen split open with a sharp cracking sound. Three deer sheltering under overhanging branches of a large cedar, thinking that the sound was a rifle shot, bolted from their refuge and fled through the chest-high snow, finally stopping when exhaustion from plowing through the heavy drifts overcame them. With ears erect, heads swiveling, ever alert, they gasped deep breaths of cold air into their lungs, gathering strength to continue their flight. No ominous figures stirred, the dead-calm air carried no scent of danger, and as the pale winter sun pushed its way above the southeastern horizon and shed its anemic light on a scene of peace, the deer relaxed and began to browse, storing up energy toward the long frigid night.

In other areas, predators searched for cold-weakened prey. Life — and death — went on in the silent winter wilderness.

*   *   *

Herb Schultz's head was thick and throbbing from his usual Saturday night in the Deerhorn Tavern when he stumbled out of bed. Age was taking its toll. This morning he considered that he still felt as hung over as he had in the old days, on half the amount of booze. He couldn't hold as much as he used to when he was younger, and when Carl Nelson had said he was going home early because he might not be able to get up the hill if the snow got too deep, Herb willingly abandoned the company of other drinkers and rode home with Carl. Carl let Herb off in front of his shack before turning into his own driveway opposite. Herb's battered old gray Ford pickup absolutely refused to start in cold weather, so he had taken out the battery, drained the oil, and left it for the winter. He could usually bum a ride with someone.

It was not the early morning light that got him up, but the urgent need to piss. He staggered into the makeshift bathroom, made by walling off a portion of the porch, relieved himself, then returned to his bedroom to pull wool pants over his long johns and slide his stockinged feet into old, battered slippers. He looked into the wood-burning kitchen stove, found the fire completely out, and shoved newspaper and kindling into the fire box. His hand was shaky as he struck a kitchen match and lit the paper.

Good thing he'd hung onto this old stove, he told himself. His sister Edna, when she'd married her second husband, now, they'd built themselves a big fancy house over to Cottonwood, on the breaks of the Salmon Canyon. All electric. Not even a fireplace. But then, even them oil furnaces had to have power to turn them on. Funny place to build a house anyway. No trees nowhere about, except there must have been one somewhere because a couple of years ago, one had fallen across the power line in a blizzard, and being as how they was way to hell and gone out in the sticks, that was the last place the power crews got around to fixing. Took them three days. Like to froze, they did, Edna and her man. Had to move in with the neighbors.

Herb reflected that the two-burner hot plate sitting on the kitchen counter was enough to cook on in the summer when it was too hot to build a fire. His cooking talents were simple anyway, consisting of making coffee, frying bacon and eggs, and heating up cans of stuff. He had never bothered to ponder the drawbacks of sawing, splitting and carrying wood for the stove. He had always worked in the woods. Saws and axes felt normal to his hands. He had an oil stove for heat, but had run out of oil to burn in it. All the dealers knew him and not a one would give him credit, so he'd have to wait for his next Social Security check before he could fill the tank.

When he was sure the fire would burn, he found cigarette papers and a pouch of cheap tobacco. He extracted one of the flimsy papers, his thick, work-callused fingers having difficulty separating one piece from the others. He made a groove of the paper and shook tobacco into it, his hand shaking, not entirely from the cold. He licked the edge of the paper and with a flick of his left index finger, rolled it into a tube. He twisted the ends, placed one end in his mouth, then removing a stove lid, inserted a sliver of kindling into the fire and transferred the flame to the end of his cigarette. He inhaled deeply. Only then did he begin to feel human.

He remembered his bitch, Queenie, and her five pups in the big box on the walled-in porch, and went to look at her. Immediately he knew he wasn't going to be able to go back to bed and sleep off his hangover. The pups, whose eyes were just beginning to open, were making a racket, and Queenie whimpered anxiously as tremors shook her body.

"Damn it all to hell," Herb growled. "She's gonna have that damn milk fever again. I'll hafta git a vet. Can't git old George. He won't be no more sober than I am. Not that snot-nosed kid what works with him neither. I'll call the Merrill girl. She'll come. Damn, I oughta get that dog spaded, but those goddam vets want so much for it."

Herb pulled on extra socks, boots, two flannel shirts, a red and black checked wool jacket and a green and black checked wool cap with flaps down over the ears. He debated his options. He had no phone, so he would have to hike in the snow to a neighbor's house.

Not old Eugene, he thought. *Can't go there.* Eugene Pettijohn's property adjoined Herb's, down the road a ways. Where Herb was a dirty old man, dressed in worn clothing of cheap manufacture, his grizzled black-turning-gray hair uncombed, a rough stubble perpetually covering his chin, Eugene was neat and tidy, well dressed in pricey clothing and expensive boots. His sleek gray hair was always neatly combed, his chin smoothly shaven. Herb was a logger. Eugene was a forester. There is a world of difference. Eugene's property, a log cabin and a new, prefabricated sheet-metal barn, bordered the road, the woodlot behind doubling as pasture for a cow and calf. Eugene's fences consisted of tightly strung woven wire fastened to solidly set metal posts. He'd even put a fence on his side of the line between his property and Herb's, even though Herb had a three-strand barbed wire fence there. Herb's split cedar fence posts were rotting; some had fallen over, leaving the wire slack. Some of the posts were held up only by the connecting strands. Still, it annoyed him that Eugene had put up another fence. The two neighbors rarely spoke.

No, he'd have to go down to Jess Dibble's. Jess would be out, driving the snow plow, which meant that the road up Black Bear Ridge would be the first one plowed, but his wife Jackie would be working in her kitchen. Nice woman, Jackie. Always willing to help someone.

A truck with chains on the rear dual wheels had passed down the road, leaving tracks that made walking easier. Herb noted that Carl hadn't gotten very far up his driveway last night. He'd left his pickup truck where it had gotten stuck in a dip in the lane and walked on in to his mobile home, his tracks barely visible where the snow had fallen into them. A big ox of a Swede, he wouldn't have had any trouble getting on down the lane to his place.

As Herb neared Eugene's neat farmyard, he became aware of another animal in distress. Eugene's cow was bawling her head off and her calf was adding to the ruckus. Herb stopped opposite the barn. The cow was inside, the door hadn't been opened this morning since the snow lay up against it undisturbed. There were no tracks leading from Eugene's house to the barn. Strange, that. Eugene always milked the cow at six AM. You could set your watch by it. It was now getting on toward eight.

Herb swung the gate of the barnyard open; a neat metal-barred gate that moved on well-oiled hinges, not like the rickety gates on most folk's property. He pushed back the sliding door enough to let himself in. The cow, a freckled red and white Milking Shorthorn, stamped her feet and paced restlessly, stopping only momentarily to glare at Herb as if accusing him of causing her plight. The human intrusion brought an increase in the volume of the calf's complaint as it tried to push through the partition between itself and the cow. Herb noted the cow's distended udder, causing her to walk spraddle-legged. Small streams of milk squirted from the teats as the cow moved.

Herb left the barn and retraced his steps to the road. At the gate to Eugene's front yard, he hesitated, then reluctantly pushed the gate open and waded through the pristine snow to the front door, which stood ajar. He peered inside.

There was old Eugene, sitting there staring at him, stone cold dead, a bullet hole in his chest.

The interior of the room was as cold as it was outside, there were only dead white ashes in the fireplace, and a glass of water on a small table beside Eugene's easy chair was frozen solid.

Fighting down his aversion to dead bodies, Herb entered the room, staying next to the wall and giving the body a wide berth as he sidled toward the door to the kitchen. Herb had worked in the woods all his life and had seen dead men there; men who had been crushed by falling trees, men who had been mangled by machinery, men who had been knifed in barroom brawls. He'd been in the army in Korea, where they had been ambushed and pinned down by Chink machine gunners located in the hills above them, and had died like flies. The freshly dead didn't bother him. It was the cold, stiff ones that did. It was a cultural thing, borne of childhood admonitions not to go near graveyards. He was as superstitious as the next man, and even hated to look on the dolled-up dead lying in their coffins.

It was a relief to make it to the kitchen, where he found the stainless steel milk pail, spotlessly clean, upended on the sink drain board. He went out the back door and slogged through the snow to the barn. There he fastened the cow into her stanchion, threw a flake of hay—good alfalfa, he noted — into her manger, forked some to the calf, dipped out a scoop of grain and checked that the heated cups of the automatic waterer were working so the animals' water was not frozen. Finding the stool, he sat down to milk her. His coarse hands were rough, not like Eugene's soft, gentle ones, and his technique was rusty, but one never forgets how to do it. The cow kicked at his first attempts, but he talked to her, and realizing that she soon would feel better, she settled down. Herb took half a pail of milk, which flowed into the bucket in a steamy froth. He loosened the stanchion and turned the calf in with the cow to finish the job of emptying her udder.

He didn't go back to Eugene's house. He carried the pail of milk out to the road and headed back toward his shack. True to form, Jess Dibble had been by with the snowplow, and the walking was easier.

Herb got Queenie to drink some of the milk and forced some down each of the pups. Then he set off again, down the road to the Dibble place. He was not about to go back into Eugene's house and look at that stiff again!

He had never gotten himself a phone and like a lot of older people, felt uncomfortable with them, especially these newfangled touch-tone ones. He hadn't brought his reading glasses, but the youngest Dibble, nine-year-old Eddie Lee, looked up the numbers and read them out while he hesitantly dialed them.

He called Dr. Erica Merrill first.

Only then did he call the sheriff.

*   *   *

The previous evening, a Saturday in mid-January, Dr. Erica Merrill and the town's other two veterinarians had gone down the river to Lincoln to attend a meeting of their area veterinary association. The featured speaker was an expert in contagious diseases from the vet school at Washington State University. Erica and Trent Somers, another young vet who one day would take over George McLeod's practice, listened intently to a discussion of heartworm and Lyme disease, but George, bored by the topic, wandered off in search of the bar.

By the time the meeting broke up, George was about as tight as the blood-filled ticks that spread the Lyme disease organism. Erica and Trent shoe-horned him into the back seat of Trent's low-slung sports car, a novelty in their small backwater town. They headed up the river, making time. Normally Erica objected to the speed at which Trent drove, especially on the winding road in the dark canyon with the river running swift and black only feet away. But the weather report on the car radio told them they were racing a fast-moving cold front and she did not relish the thought of having it catch up with them.

At around ten o'clock, they decanted George from the back seat and left him in the capable hands of his wife, Maureen. They declined her invitation to come in for a cup of coffee. Snow was beginning to fall in isolated flakes, slowly drifting down, and they were anxious to get home before it started snowing in earnest. They turned back onto the river highway, crossed the bridge over Boulder Creek, and turned east up the road to Boulder, county seat of Mountain County in North Central Idaho. Running the three miles up the creek, they reached the outskirts of Boulder, and the large rambling house that had been in the Merrill family for three generations. Erica shared it with her grandmother, and used part of the basement for her veterinary clinic.

Trent wheeled the snappy red car around in a tire-squealing U turn, lurching to a stop beside the front walk.

"I'll just let you out and go. I'd better get up the hill before it starts snowing hard. These tires aren't any good in snow."

They'd probably be better. Erica mused uncharitably, if Trent didn't burn the tread off them with his sudden stops, starts and turns. There was at least one small consolation with the unpleasant weather forecast. Trent hadn't made his usual unwelcome pass at her. She jumped out before he could change his mind, and bending double so she could look back through the open door, gave Trent a smile of cloying sweetness. "Thanks for the ride," she said and slammed the door. Trent jerked the gas-burner into gear and screamed away.

The large, white, two-story house stood in sharp contrast to the box-like houses, the shacks and the trailers of most of the residents of Boulder. Some larger houses built in recent years were of the low-slung ranch type. Only a few older houses matched the Merrill home — the Glasers', the Vanderpools', the Matsons' and the McMurtrys'. The house had dormer windows on the upper floor, a full basement, and huge rooms on the ground floor. Even with Erica's clinic occupying much of the basement, there was more room than she and her grandmother really needed. A neat white picket fence surrounded the house, huge sycamore trees overhung the south-facing facade and a productive vegetable garden occupied most of the back yard. Gram's neatly tended flower borders were now a wasteland of dead stems, but would bloom again in the early spring with crocuses, daffodils and tulips.

A neat, white sign hung limply from its standard, its brown lettering proclaiming the east end of the house to be the "Merrill Animal Hospital, Erica Merrill, D.V.M." An arrow pointed the way to the basement door where the designation was repeated in black letters on the frosted glass. Erica was proud of this. It had meant years of hard work and financial sacrifice, but finally, four years after graduating from vet school, she had hung up this sign and started her own practice here in her home town. She hoped she had the maturity and self-assurance to make it a success, but was still struggling, awaiting acceptance from the rural population who thought of vets as men and still referred to her as "Hugh Merrill's girl."

As she admired the sign, a gust of wind caught it and whipped it out almost horizontal. Flakes of snow swirled round her, falling thick and heavy. She scurried up the flagstone walk to the house and let herself in.

"Is that you, Erica?"

"Yes, Gram."

"You're late. Mrs. Rushmore called and I told her you'd be back at ten."

Erica pushed up the cuff of her parka and glanced at her watch. "It's only ten after."

"It's still late. You'll have to be prompt if you want to stay in business."

Erica rolled her eyes heavenward, remembering the hours they had sometimes waited on the Merrill ranch for George McLeod to make it out there to treat one of their animals. She picked up the phone to call Mrs. Rushmore. She knew what the call would be about. Mrs. R would want to leave her cat for boarding and would insist that, since Erica lived at her clinic, she should take the cat in on Sunday. Hardly an urgent call. She was right, too; that's exactly what the call was about.

Then with the storm raging beyond the well-insulated walls, Erica took herself off to bed, with no inkling of what lay in store for her on the morrow.

CHAPTER 2

Erica Merrill, her slender five-foot-four frame clad in pajamas, robe and wool-lined slippers, tucked her feet under her in a big chair before the fireplace to read the newspaper. Sounds of activity came from the kitchen, Gram's domain, which Erica was seldom allowed to invade. In exchange for tasty, balanced meals, something Erica herself was not good at preparing, she did the heavier work around the house. It was Gram's house and Erica paid monthly rent to use part of it for her clinic.

Erica's grandfather, Marcus Merrill, Gram's husband, had built the house back in the thirties when it had seemed practical to have a house in town as well as the one on the ranch. Lumber was cheap in those days and there were enough sturdy young Merrills to build it without having to hire outside help. Gram and Gramp, Clara and Marcus to everyone else, had moved into it after the ranch had been turned over to the sons. Gramp had died two years ago, having lived long enough to see his granddaughter graduate with honors from vet school, something that he viewed with wonder and pride. Erica's father, Hugh, was now running the ranch. Hugh's son, Wade, Erica's older brother, was taking more and more of the responsibility.

The land on what was now called Merrill Bench had been homesteaded in 1900 by the first of the Idaho Merrills, William, and his wife, Judith. That land was still in the family and had been added to by the acquisition of neighboring ranches. The entire Bench now belonged to the

Merrills and consisted of three ranches, each occupied by a different family member. Wade and Erica were fourth generation Merrills, and Wade's two toddlers, William Hugh, aged three and Marcus Wade, aged eighteen months were the fifth.

The rich farmland of Merrill Bench, bounded on the west by the Whitewater River and on the south by Boulder Creek, sloped gradually upward toward the foothills of the Bitterroot Mountains. From its upper parts one could look southwestward and see the rolling hills of the Palouse country, pale yellow in summertime from the fields of wheat. Directly west, across the river, were low, timbered mountains. To the south, across Boulder Creek, a mirror-image bench, named after another pioneer, Henry Laird, sloped up toward another timbered ridge. Behind Boulder, the mountains began in earnest, rising in ever-higher ridges to the Continental Divide. Mountain County, though not the largest in the state of Idaho, was nevertheless larger than two of the nation's smaller states. The population was sparse and mostly clustered around Boulder and along the river. Farm animals outnumbered people, and no one had ever tried to count the wildlife. More than ninety percent of the land was timbered, and only along the river and in a few mountain meadows was there land worth farming. In Boulder itself, the farmers and the loggers had lived in uneasy truce for nearly a century.

The low-pitched tone of a phone alerted Erica to a call for her services. The other phone was turned up to maximum volume so Gram could hear it. Gram usually didn't notice the business phone unless she happened to be passing by when it rang. Erica had told her many times that she needn't answer it, and wished fervently that she would not, but Gram came from that generation that took responsibility seriously, and would never ignore a ringing phone.

Erica uncoiled from the chair, a frown on her triangular face with its widely set brown eyes, straight nose and thin-lipped mouth. She pushed her short, wavy dark brown hair back from her forehead, and went to the little alcove in the hall where the phone was kept.

"Dr. Merrill speaking."

As soon as the speaker identified himself, Erica groaned. This time she wished Gram had answered it, but then realized that to ask Gram to fib about whether Erica was available would have gotten her nowhere. She was stuck. What did he want this time? Herb Schultz still owed her for a call six months ago to treat his bitch for eclampsia. When she heard him say that he had the same problem again, Erica moaned anew. While casting about for a polite way to say no to him, she heard him say, "You'll hafta come up to the house. I ain't got no car. 'Sides, ole Eugene Pettijohn is dead and I gotta call the sheriff. You know them guys. They'll keep me tied up till hell freezes over, so I left the place unlocked. You'll hafta just go up there and give her a shot."

Thinking that it wouldn't take very long for hell to freeze over in this weather, Erica realized that she had been neatly corralled. Neither of the other vets would go; she was sure of that. The dog desperately needed treatment. The deadbeat owner had a valid reason not to be there to pay her.

Erica popped her head into the kitchen and said to Gram, "I have to go out to Herb Schultz'. Queenie's having eclampsia again. I wish he'd get that dog spayed so she wouldn't keep on going through this."

"He still owes you for the last time."

"I know. But I have to treat her."

"Have him bring her in. Then make him pay for both times before he takes her home."

"I'd like to, but he says he can't bring her in. I don't have any choice."

"You'll never make a living that way, Erey. You're too soft."

How true that was. Erica knew she was a pushover for anyone with a sob story, but she hadn't figured out how to get around it. She always thought of the animal first, not of the money. All the deadbeats in town, who were known and not welcomed at George McLeod's Riverside Clinic, were trying her out. Before long they'd all owe her money.

Erica dressed warmly in a sweat suit topped by a ski sweater and went into her clinic to put supplies she would need into her medical bag. Donning a green and purple snowmobile outfit that her brother Wade had given her for Christmas, she shoveled the driveway and the walk, as her blue Jeep Cherokee warmed up. She decided against putting on chains. The road up Black Bear Ridge would be plowed, and she had good snow tires.

The ridge was formed by Boulder Creek, tumbling through its giant canyon on the north, and Black Bear Creek, more commonly shortened to Bear Creek, angling off in a southeasterly direction. If you followed the road back into the mountains, had a four-wheel-drive vehicle, and it was in the late summer, you could drive all the way over the Continental Divide into Montana, following an old Indian trail. The nearer part of the road was heavily traveled by monster logging trucks, hauling the remains of the once mighty forests out of the now denuded mountains. It was a good road, and well traveled, and true to form, had been efficiently plowed. Erica had no trouble getting up onto the ridge, and when she came to Herb's shack, she turned into his driveway and gunned the Cherokee until the rear end had cleared the road. There she stopped. She'd have no trouble backing down out of the drive if she didn't try to go any farther.

She noticed as she passed that a lone sheriff's car stood in front of Eugene Pettijohn's neat log cabin. Wondering how he had died, she reckoned that it must have been some sort of an accident for the law to become involved. Eugene had been a client. He was miserly, always questioning her fee, but he always paid. That and the fact that he also followed her instructions to the letter had made her place him in the category of "good" clients. He had been one of the few clients around Boulder who had enough of an education to understand what she was talking about. She would miss him.

Erica went to the back door of Herb's shack, following rural etiquette borne of the fact that country people lived in their kitchens, and in winter frequently shut off the parts of their houses they did not need to heat. The door onto the back porch was unlocked and Herb had left the one into the kitchen open. The first thing Erica did, after noting that Queenie, a medium-sized black and white long-haired dog of indeterminate origin, was indeed showing mild seizures, was to open the wood-burning kitchen range and fill the firebox with fresh pieces of wood. When she was sure they would burn, she returned to the back porch.

Queenie was a friendly dog and licked Erica's hand as she reached into the whelping box to move Queenie to a spot where it would be easier to work on her. Erica opened her bag, selected a syringe and needle, drew calcium solution into the syringe, scissored hair from Queenie's foreleg over the vein, applied a tourniquet and cleaned the skin with alcohol. The vein stood out plainly, as large and firm as a pencil because of the increased blood pressure caused by the muscular effort of Queenie's seizures. Erica had no trouble inserting the needle into the vein, in spite of the poor light in the cramped room.

As she slowly injected the calcium solution, she watched the dog's muscles relax, her panting stop and her anxious expression disappear. Finally, Queenie heaved a great sigh, rolled onto her side, stretched, gave a satisfied grunt, and seemed willing to lie quietly and rest. Erica turned her attention to the pups. When she picked one up, it let out a cry and Queenie jumped to her feet and trotted back to the box. Erica let her get into the box and nurse her puppies, though she would have preferred to separate them in order to stop the drain of calcium from the bitch's body. However, the pups needed the warmth of their mother. It was cold on the porch in spite of the open door into the kitchen.

Erica had noticed a pail of milk sitting on the kitchen table. She returned to the kitchen, where the fire was now roaring in the stove, and looked around for a clean kettle to warm some of the milk. Not finding anything clean, she rinsed out a coffee pot in which the residue of many helpings of thick, black coffee clung to the sides and bottom. She couldn't get it entirely clean; the pups would have to have a bit of coffee in their milk. Putting the pot on the stove, she warmed the milk and filled a small pet nursing bottle she had brought. Then taking the pups one at a time, she let them fill their stomachs.

Should she leave the puppy formula she had brought, or just tell Herb to feed them the cow's milk? The formula was expensive and she had no faith that she would receive any more payment for this call than for the last one. She hadn't expected to find fresh milk in Herb's house. Canned milk perhaps, but the fresh milk was a bonus. She wondered where it had come from. She decided not to leave the formula, at least until she had talked to Herb and extracted some money from him. He'd probably be down at Eugene's. If not, he'd be at the Dibbles'.

She filled a pill vial with calcium tablets, wrote instructions on the label, rinsed out the coffee pot, which Herb would probably now think had been ruined, and put more wood into the stove. Herb had the living room of his shack shut off, with an old gunny sack stuck under the door to prevent drafts. Erica had seen an oil tank outside along the living room wall. Herb must be out of oil for the heating stove in the front room and unable to afford more. There was only one bedroom, and if there was a closet, it wasn't there. Herb's dirty clothes (it didn't look as if he had any clean ones) were thrown on the foot of the bed or on the floor. The place stank of spoiled food and human sweat, and Erica was reminded that before it began to smell of dog poop, she'd better let Queenie out.

While Queenie was doing her business outside, Erica wrote up a bill for her services. She was about to leave it on the table, but assumed that she'd find Herb next door and decided to take it with her. She needed to talk to Herb anyway.

The puppies were now sleeping peacefully, their fat bellies full of warm milk, and Queenie nuzzled Erica's hand affectionately when Erica reached into the box. There was no sign of further tremors. Erica let herself out into the cold and carefully shut the rickety door behind her.

As she backed out of Herb's drive, she saw that there was now a lot of activity at Eugene's place. Two brown sheriff's cars were parked outside, one with its red and blue lights flashing. An ambulance had arrived and its flashing red light added to the brilliance of the scene. There were several other cars. A crowd was beginning to gather in spite of the cold, and a brown-clad deputy sheriff was half-heartedly shooing the onlookers away. Erica had to park up by Eugene's barn and walk down to the house.

The Pettijohn place stood out from its neighbors like an orchid in a dandelion patch. The cabin, built by a professional, sat in a neatly tended lawn surrounded by a split rail fence. Woven wire fences, supported by steel posts enclosed the barnyard and pasture. The barn was a prefabricated metal one with room for two cows, a separate pen for calves, and an equipment room on one side; the other side being devoted to hay storage. Everything was neat and in its place. Manure was removed daily, and sawdust, a common commodity in a lumber town, was spread on the floor of the animals' pens.

The deputy met her at the gate. "Hi there, Erica. Out on an early call?"

"Yes. Is Herb Schultz there?" She motioned toward the group of men crowded onto Eugene's porch.

"Yeah, he is. Why?"

"I've been up to his place to treat his dog. I need to talk to him."

"How'd you know he'd be here?"

"He told me over the phone when he called me about the dog that Eugene was dead and he was going to call you."

"Oh, I see. Did he call you on Eugene's phone?"

"No, I don't think so. I think he was calling from the Dibbles'. Why?"

The deputy didn't answer, but told Erica to wait outside the gate, which he closed firmly before walking by a circuitous route up to the porch. A well-beaten path had been made in the snow, off to the side of the walk. Leading up the walk was one single set of prints, clear and clean, in the sparkling snow.

The deputy, a man named Walt Forgey, shouldered his way through the group on the porch, and in a moment Erica saw the tall figure of the sheriff, Pete Torgeson, in his trademark Stetson, appear in the open doorway of the house, look toward her, and confer with Forgey and with a man clad in black wool pants and a red and black checked coat. This man half turned his head and Erica recognized him as Herb Schultz. She assumed that he would come out to the gate to talk to her. But it was Forgey who returned to the gate, opened it and said, "Go on up. Herb's on the porch. Don't walk up the path direct. Keep over there to the side."

Something unusual was happening, Erica realized, and with a tight feeling in the pit of her stomach, acutely aware of everything around her, she made her way up the beaten trail and climbed the two steps up onto the porch. Men moved back slightly to make room for her and she found herself looking into the living room of Eugene Pettijohn's neat log cabin at an astonishing sight.

CHAPTER 3

Erica's eyes surveyed the scene while her mind photographed it for her memory. Eugene Pettijohn's body was slumped in a sitting position, leaning against one side of the fireplace, the head canted to the left with the open eyes staring straight ahead. The mouth, unencumbered by his dentures, hung open. An astonished expression was frozen on the face. A dark red stain surrounded a small neat hole in the middle of the chest, the only thing to mar the neat cleanliness of his creamy white wool underwear. He had removed his shirt and was clad in trousers, held up by suspenders, over his long johns. Blood on the floor and on the rough stone of the fireplace just above his head indicated that he had been standing when he had been shot, the impact of the bullet had knocked him back against the fireplace, his slippered feet had slid forward, wrinkling the Navajo rug, and his body had slumped into a sitting position on the hardwood floor. Erica realized that she'd just as soon not see the exit wound, which must have been a mess of ripped flesh and bone, clotted blood, and torn clothing. It must have been a large caliber bullet that had hit him, yet from the front, Eugene in death looked almost as neat as he had in life.

Maybe that neatness was part of the reason people didn't like him. Eugene dressed in precisely creased dark green whipcord trousers and jacket, Pendleton shirts of pure wool, and expensive hiking boots, kept clean and supple with neatsfoot oil. Though he worked in the woods, he disdained the usual logger garb of heavy jeans, T shirts in summer and flannel shirts in winter, and heavy, cleated-soled boots kept waterproof with applications of stuff that looked like axle grease. No logger worth his salt ever looked neat, let alone clean. They always reminded Erica of her college chemistry professor who said he liked to see messy, acid-stained student lab notebooks. It showed him they'd been working.

Eugene was a forester, something else that bugged the locals. His consulting business, which he offered to the new breed of landowner, a more environmentally conscious bunch, was heavy on conservation, on tree farming rather than slashing down anything marketable. He thought of the future of the forest, where the locals thought of the next job. Erica remembered telling one of her clients about a trip to an area of British Columbia, up in Canada, which still had vast tracts of virgin timber. To her amazement, the client hadn't been impressed. To his way of thinking, virgin timber was equated with unemployment. Erica herself tended to agree with Eugene Pettijohn's way of thinking.

She had liked Eugene, in spite of his tight purse strings and his almost total lack of humor. He rarely smiled, and a compliment from him was such a rarity, that the one time she had received one, she had considered it a great honor.

Clay Caldwell, a tall young man of husky build, in the brown uniform of a deputy sheriff, looked up briefly from his careful examination of the floor, smiled and said, "Hi, Erica."

"Hello, Clay. What are you looking for?"

"Evidence," Clay stated, applying himself once more to his work.

"That's evident," Erica punned. "What specifically?"

Clay didn't answer her, but directed his next remark to Pete Torgeson. "Here's the slug." Clay fingered the spent bullet that he held in his left hand as he rocked back on his heels. He tossed it gently into the air and caught it again, judging its heft as well as its size. "I'd say it was from a thirty-thirty or a thirty-ought-six, but it's too flattened from hitting the stone wall to get any rifling marks off of it."

Torgeson frowned. "So you won't be able to tell what rifle fired it?"

"That's right."

"It *would* have to be a common caliber of gun. Ninety percent of the homes in this county have one or the other of them."

Clay grinned. "Well, at least that gives us lots of suspects."

Torgeson snorted, not seeing the humor. Then remembering Erica, he turned to her. "What do you want with Herb?"

"He called me to come out and treat his dog. I need to talk to him about her."

Torgeson glanced over his shoulder at the small group of men on the porch. "You'll have to ask Kline."

But before she could do so, two men from the local mortuary arrived on the porch, bearing a stretcher. The older of the two leading the way, paused at the open door, glanced inside, and seeing Clay on his hands and knees still searching for evidence, demanded, "You haven't disturbed the body have you?"

Clay, recognizing the undertaker as the local coroner, replied, "No sir. I've left him just the way he was and I've told everyone else to stay out of the room."

"Well, don't touch him. The body's my business."

"Yes sir. But before you take him away, I need to take some pictures. I'll want some of his back."

"We will preserve any evidence we find," the coroner replied haughtily. He turned toward his assistant and while his back was turned, Clay made a small gesture in his direction that Erica interpreted as one of contempt. He grinned at her, a mischievous look in his gray eyes, and she returned the smile. In high school, she had dated Clay, but they'd gone their separate ways, she to the University of Idaho and then to vet school at Washington State, he to

Boise State University. She liked him and wondered if they would ever pick up the relationship again. He wasn't married, she knew. He was the only young man in Boulder that she could generate even the faintest interest in. Compared with Trent Somers, Clay Caldwell rated a lot higher on the Richter scale.

The two undertakers, both wearing heavy black overcoats over shiny black suits of cheap material, rolled their stretcher to a point near the body. The coroner reached out and touched the stiffened corpse and intoned solemnly, "I declare this man dead." He paused for dramatic effect, but this not being news to anyone else, failed to have any impact on them. When the men lifted the body onto the stretcher, they tried to lay it on its back, but it was literally frozen into a sitting position and toppled over, falling to the floor with a loud thud and causing the stretcher to skitter away. Before the men could retrieve the stretcher and return to their task, Clay began to photograph the exit wound.

"Get away from there!" the coroner snarled. "The body's my business."

"The evidence is mine," Clay responded.

"I told you we'd save anything we find."

Erica saw the slight shift of Clay's focus, catching the meaningful glare from the sheriff. Clay said mildly, "Yes sir."

"Here, help us get this body on the stretcher," the coroner demanded.

Clay gave them a hand, lifting the body, which was quite light — Eugene was not a large man — and laying it this time on its side. The younger man from the mortuary reverently placed a blanket over the corpse. They wheeled the stretcher to the door, where Walt Forgey helped carry it out to the hearse, which had replaced the unneeded ambulance near the front gate. The coroner turned in the doorway and asked, "Where are his dentures? I want to take them."

Clay answered, "They're in the bathroom but you can't take them yet. Not till I get all the evidence from the house." In an aside to Erica and Torgeson, he muttered, "Besides, they're in a cup of water that's frozen solid."

The Coroner seemed on the verge of raising an objection, but Pete Torgeson intervened. "We have to preserve the crime scene until we've gone over it thoroughly. You won't be able to get them back in his mouth until you thaw him out anyway."

"Just make sure I get them."

"We will."

While this was going on, Erica had managed to remain quietly on the edge of the group, observing everything without calling attention to herself. Now Torgeson noticed her once more and said, "Go talk to Kline."

"Herb's the one I want to talk to."

"Yeah, I know. But he's Kline's prisoner."

"What?"

"Just talk to Kline," Torgeson responded roughly.

Erica stepped away from the doorway and turned toward a small group of men standing a few paces from the door. One was a short, man who had never built up any muscle mass to cover his bones and who was running to flab in spite of his small stature. Dressed nattily in business suit and tie, dress shoes with raised heels to make him seem taller, and a lined raincoat, he looked as if he was freezing. His ears were reddened, his hands shoved deep into his pockets, his lips blue. Yet he kept a beady eye on the impassive logger lounging against the porch railing. Walt Forgey had returned from carrying out the body and was also watching the logger. The small man Erica recognized as the county attorney, Lyle Kline. With distaste, because she hadn't liked him ever since he had campaigned for the office and had taken it away from Otis Vanderpool, Erica went up to him and stated that she needed to talk to Herb.

"He isn't allowed to talk to anyone but us."

"Why?" Erica asked an unnecessary question just to needle Kline.

"He's under arrest for first degree murder."

"I didn't shoot the old geezer," the logger growled.

"You shut up." Kline turned toward Erica. "Who are you and what do you want with him?"

"I'm Doctor Erica Merrill. I'm a veterinarian. Herb called me to come treat his dog and I need to talk to him." She put a subtle emphasis on the word "Doctor."

"We're dealing with more important things than some dog."

"No you aren't. Eugene's dead. There's nothing urgent about him. The dog is sick and needs care."

"Damn right. That's what I been tellin' ya," Herb argued in a throaty grumble.

"Well, make it snappy. It's cold out here and I'm tired of hanging around." Kline was trying unsuccessfully to keep from shivering.

Erica turned toward the logger. A next-door neighbor to Eugene Pettijohn, he couldn't have been any more of a contrast to that man if he had deliberately tried. He was about six feet tall, broad-shouldered and barrel-chested. You could sense his muscular power even under the layers of winter clothing. He took his cap off to scratch his head. He had stiff black hair, beginning to turn grey, that wouldn't lie down flat, a thick black stubble on his jutting jaw, heavy black eyebrows on his ridgy forehead, and black hair growing out of his ear canals and his nostrils. Yet he might have been attractive to a certain kind of girl in his younger days, with his physique and his rugged jaw line.

His red and black checked wool jacket had seen better days, the collars of two flannel shirts, layered one over the other, were filthy, and the neckline of his once white cotton underwear was frayed and dirty gray, with the top button missing. Black chest hair flowed out of the opening. He owed her money. He was an irresponsible dog owner in that he didn't get his dog spayed or vaccinated. So why did she suddenly want to side with him against Kline, the county attorney?

Because he had called her first when Queenie got sick? Or because anything Kline did, she told herself, was bound to be wrong? She did not want Kline to succeed.

She told Herb she had given Queenie a calcium injection, that Queenie would need calcium tablets and that the pups needed to have supplementary feeding, but because of the cold they needed to be with their mother for warmth. Herb nodded and glanced sideways at Kline.

"Where he's going, he won't be able to do any of that," Kline asserted.

"I'll have to take her down to the clinic then," Erica told Herb. "I'd like to have payment for my services so far and some in advance for boarding her."

Herb shrugged. "I ain't got no money on me."

"We'll take care of them pups," a treble voice chimed in. The people in the group turned and looked down over the edge of the porch to see Eddie Lee Dibble, with his mother, Jackie, laboring through the snow in his wake. They'd done an end run around Walt Forgey's security and blazed a trail through the snow on the lower side of the house. "Won't we, Mom?" Eddie Lee turned toward his mother.

"Won't we what?"

"Take care of Mr. Schultz's dog and her puppies."

"Why can't he do it himself?"

"I dunno." Eddie Lee had missed that part of the story.

"Because he's being arrested for murder," Kline said, unnecessarily loudly.

Jackie gasped and stared at Herb, who stared back.

"We can take care of Queenie, can't we?" Eddie Lee demanded, not at all interested in murder.

"I guess so," Jackie puffed. "One more litter of dogs around the place won't make much difference."

"Just why is Herb being arrested?" Erica asked curtly. Everyone turned toward Kline with questioning looks.

"Because he didn't like the decedent and constantly quarreled with him. Because he owns the kind of gun that killed Pettijohn. Because he called us with a cock-and-bull story about finding Pettijohn dead, but going off and milking a cow and feeding his dog before he even called us."

"Ol' Eugene was dead. He weren't goin' nowhere. Cow's gotta be milked at the right time. An' I knew onct I called you guys, my bitch'd be dead afore you let me git the vet."

That even silenced Kline, though his reaction was more one of perplexity, of trying to figure out what Herb was talking about. The rest of the people understood perfectly. And whether they wanted to admit it or not, they agreed.

Kline hadn't gotten it figured out well enough to mount a response, but as everyone was waiting on him, he covered up by blustering. "Who asked you to say anything. You keep your mouth shut. Forgey, let's take him in."

Walt Forgey flicked a glance at Pete Torgeson, who nodded, so Walt escorted Herb Schultz out to the sheriff's car, with Kline a safe distance in the rear. Kline waited until Forgey had seated Herb in the back seat and shut the door before approaching the car and sliding into the passenger side.

Torgeson had stepped into the living room of the cabin, standing just inside the door. He said to Clay, "Eugene's gun is back on the rack. I thought he'd taken it over to Sarah's to lock away so the kid couldn't get at it."

"Yeah, that's what I heard. It's his gun all right. There aren't two like it around here."

The two men eyed the ancient lever-action Winchester 30.30 with reverence. It was a beautiful gun. Probably over one hundred years old, it had an octagonal barrel, shined to a high polish. A wilderness scene had been carved into the metal and a similar design carved into the wood of the stock. The silver butt plate carried the initials, E P in elaborate script.

"Whoever cleaned it last did a sloppy job," Torgeson commented.

"That must have been Ronnie," Clay mused, speaking of the fifteen-year-old nephew, Ronnie Bixby, who lived with Eugene. "Pettijohn would have made him do a better job once he saw it, I bet."

"Yeah. I wonder where Ronnie is."

"He's not in the house. I looked everywhere; even under the beds and in the attic. I wanted to see whether he was another victim, or whether he might have done the shooting and was holed up somewhere in the house."

"Did you think he might have done it?"

Clay shrugged. "It seemed like a good possibility right at first. Now it doesn't look like it."

"We've got to find him. Maybe Sarah knows."

Clay shook his head. "She's the last person who'd know what that kid was up to."

"Yeah, you're right." Torgeson half turned and seeing Erica out of the corner of his eye, whirled to face her. "What are you still doing here?"

"Eugene had a cat. It's a Siamese and has always been a house cat. Do you have any idea where she is?"

"Don't worry," Clay reassured her. "It's in the bedroom. The door's shut and the heat's on, so it's okay."

"I'd better take her back with me, unless Sarah Pettijohn wants to take her."

"That's okay by me," Torgeson replied. "Sarah is on her way over. I'm glad they got the body out of here before she came. She didn't want to drive in the snow so she got a friend to pick her up."

"What about the cow and calf?"

Torgeson groaned. "Cows! Calves! Cats! Dogs! You and your damned animals. I've got a murder on my hands and all you ask about is dogs and cats and cows."

"Okay, then. I'll ask you about the murder. How come you let Kline, who probably doesn't know what part of

31

a cow milk comes out of, accuse Herb Schultz of murder just because he stopped to milk the cow before he called you?"

Torgeson passed a hand across his face and sighed in resignation. Should he tell Erica to get lost? If he did, would she run to her daddy, the most powerful man in these parts, and tell him to back someone else for sheriff in the next election?

"Because… Clay you tell your girlfriend why we arrested Schultz."

Clay Caldwell turned beet red and swallowed hard. Did his interest in Erica show that much? Ever since Erica had returned to Boulder, he'd been trying to get up the nerve to ask her for a date, but he was afraid that her ideas of an appropriate man to date might have changed since high school days, and he always seemed to see her in the company of that other new vet, Dr. Somers. He took a deep breath.

"Well, you see, it's like this. There was only one set of tracks leading to and one set leading from this house. They were made after the snow stopped falling, and we happen to know that Eugene was alive and well and talking to his sister-in-law after the snow started to come down real heavy. Those tracks are Schultz's."

CHAPTER 4

"Are you sure he was talking to her after it started snowing?"

"She says so," Torgeson, the one who had called to break the news, replied. "She says Eugene always called her right after ten. He knew she had a favorite TV program she watched that ended at ten. She just started talking to him when she noticed the wind come up and looked out the window and saw it snowing hard. She said she ended the conversation because she wanted to get her car in the carport before the snow made it so she couldn't get up the drive."

Clay took over. "Then it would have taken him several minutes to go get his glass of water and his pills and go into the living room with them. The phone's in the kitchen."

"He took out his teeth, too," Erica said thoughtfully.

"What makes you think that? He may have taken them out earlier."

"Huh-uh. People with dentures don't like to talk without them. They mumble. I can remember calling home from college and getting Gram on the phone. She'd always make me wait, with the long-distance charges adding up, while she went and got her teeth. What kind of pills was Eugene taking?"

"Oh, just a vitamin and an antacid." Clay told her. "The bottles are in the bathroom. His teeth are in a plastic cup sort of thing with water and some cleaning stuff, but they're frozen solid."

"Speaking of freezing," Torgeson remarked, "the heat's on in the bedroom. Let's go get the cat."

"Eugene had a carrier," Erica told him. "I wonder where he kept it?"

"Let *me* look for it," Clay said hastily. "I don't want anyone else touching anything."

At the bedroom door, Erica hesitated. "I hope she won't bolt out of there. Can we shut the front door just in case?"

"How about it Clay. You done out front?"

"Yeah. Keep your hands off everything else, though. That goes for the bedroom, too. Don't move anything."

They slipped through the door one at a time, closing it quickly behind them. There was no sign of the cat. Erica, however, knew where to look. She knelt down and lifted the edge of the bedspread. Peering into the dark shadows under the bed, she saw a pair of luminous eyes.

"I see her. I think I can reach her from the back." She lay down across the bed and made a quick grab at the area the cat had been. She felt her hand touch fur, and before the cat could jump away, closed her hand around a fistful of loose skin. The cat let out a scream, but Erica hung on and pulled her from under the bed. Clay had the carrier open and Erica hastily popped the cat inside. The poor puss, a dark seal-point Siamese, shaking with fear, plastered itself against the back wall of the carrier. Erica talked soothingly and reached a finger through one of the air holes. As she touched the cat, it flinched away.

"Let's leave her in a quiet place until we're ready to take her out."

They were hailed by the young deputy who had been left by Forgey to guard the gate. "Mrs. Pettijohn's here," he called.

Torgeson shouted in reply, "Okay. Send her in but tell her not to touch anything." He opened the door for the thin, gray-haired lady who walked hesitantly into the bedroom. "Stay a minute," he murmured in Erica's ear. "As long as we're going to interview her in a bedroom, we ought to have another woman around." Erica nodded in agreement.

Sarah Pettijohn was obviously shaken by what her eyes had been unable to avoid as she walked through the front room. She asked in a tiny voice, "Do you think he died quickly? I hope he didn't suffer."

"He died instantly," Clay told her. "But I think he saw it coming. He was turned toward his assailant."

Mrs. Pettijohn quivered and collapsed onto the edge of the bed. She hid her face in her hands and Erica sat down beside her, putting an arm around her shoulders, while the two men stood by looking uncomfortable, shifting their large bodies from one foot to the other.

"Do you know who shot him?" the small, quavering voice asked.

Torgeson opened his mouth to reply, shooting a quick glance at Erica's louring countenance. He shut his mouth, then opened it and tried again. "We're still investigating."

There was a moment of silence, then Torgeson asked gently, "Do you know where Ronnie is?"

Mrs. Pettijohn shook her head. Her voice became more firm. "I wouldn't have any idea."

"Have you seen him recently?"

"He was around yesterday evening, about five-thirty or six, to pick up the gun. He's probably off somewhere shooting it."

"No. It's hanging up on the rack."

"That's good. Maybe he's getting responsible after all. I felt funny about giving it to him, anyway."

"Tell us about the gun. We heard that Eugene took it away from Ronnie."

"Yes, that's true. He thought he was too young and irresponsible to be handling a gun like that. He'd been shooting it rather recklessly, and he wasn't really supposed to shoot it at all without his permission. He was trying to give him lessons."

Erica thought that had probably galled and embarrassed the youth. What she knew of Ronnie, he was a loud-mouth and a show-off.

"So Eugene took it away from him?" Torgeson continued asking questions in a gentle, friendly voice.

"Yes. You couldn't *tell* him not to take it out and shoot it. Then it became a challenge. So he brought the gun to my house and asked me to lock it up. He didn't tell him where he'd hid it. That was last Sunday."

"But you gave it back yesterday?"

"Yes. He said that he could have it back, that he'd been punished enough. He was really soft-hearted, you know. So I had to give it back to him. Against my better judgment, mind you."

"I'm sure."

Sarah's forehead creased in a frown. She asked in a hesitant voice, "You don't think *Ronnie* did it, do you?"

"We're trying to find him to tell him about his uncle's death."

"Oh! He's not a bad boy, you know. Just not very responsible."

Sarah Pettijohn showed signs of lapsing into tears once more, so Erica, to take Sarah's mind off the tragedy, asked, "We were wondering what should be done about the cow."

"Oh, dear. I'd forgotten that. Has she been milked this morning?"

"Yes, a neighbor milked her."

"That's good. Eugene only milked her in the morning, you know. One pail of milk was more than enough for the two of us. That's why he didn't get a Holstein or some other cow that gave a lot of milk. The Shorthorn gave enough for us, and the calves were better beef quality. He took the milk we needed, then left her calf with her all day. He shut the calf in its pen last thing at night and went out to milk every morning at six. He pasteurized the milk and separated some of it, and I took most of the cream home with me to make butter." This came out in a rush of words, perhaps to keep her mind off the thought that someone had brutally murdered her brother-in-law.

Eugene Pettijohn had probably been the only milk cow owner in the county who home-pasteurized his milk. That figured. That was just like him. The Merrills got milk from the Clarkes who ran a dairy farm, and though the milk for commercial sale was now stored in bulk tanks and picked up by tanker trucks, the Clarkes still had their old pasteurizing equipment. They weren't allowed to sell milk privately, but gave it to their friends in exchange for other farm produce or for services rendered.

"I'll bet the Dibbles could use the milk. They'd probably be willing to take care of the cow," Erica suggested.

Sarah Pettijohn frowned. "They'd probably take it all and not leave any for the calf."

"I can talk to them and tell them the calf really needs it. I expect they'll cooperate. I have to see them about a litter of puppies anyway."

Sarah sighed. "All right. I guess that'll have to do."

"Also, what about the cat? We have her in a carrier."

"That thing! Well, I don't want it, if that's what you mean. Why not leave it in the barn and let the Dibbles give it some of the milk?"

"That won't do. She's a house cat. She's never been outside and she'd freeze in the barn in this weather. Besides, she needs more than milk."

"I don't suppose she'd catch mice."

"She needs more than mice, too. I'll take her down to my clinic. If you want, I'll try to find another home for her."

"All right. That's a load off my mind. There'll be a lot of other things I'll have to take care of." She started to get up.

Torgeson held up a hand. "There are a couple other questions we need to ask you. Who is the executor of Eugene's estate?"

Mrs. Pettijohn put her hand to her face and looked pensive. "I really don't know. Wilbur, my husband, was until he died. I don't know what arrangements he made after that."

"Did he have a will?"

"He did before Wilbur died, I know. Most of his estate would have gone to him. They were brothers, you know. I don't know whether he made a new will or not.

"Is Ronnie his nearest blood relative?"

"I guess so. Ronnie is his sister's son. When she and her husband were killed in a car wreck, he got stuck with him. That boy was spoiled rotten. I knew it wasn't going to work out."

"What will happen to Ronnie now? Will he live with you?"

"He will *not!* He's no blood relative of mine. I don't want anything to do with him."

"Okay. We'll let the social workers deal with that problem. Now I want to get things absolutely straight about the phone call last night. You say Eugene called you at ten o'clock each night?"

"You could set your clock by it."

"How long did you usually talk?"

"About ten minutes. He'd ask me if everything was all right. He used to tell me about all his troubles with the loggers, but I told him I wasn't interested. He and Wilbur used to talk about that for hours when they got together, but I couldn't care less."

"But you didn't talk for ten minutes this time."

"No. We'd hardly started talking when I heard this banging outside, so I pulled the curtains back and took a look. The wind had come up and it was snowing like you wouldn't believe. I told him I'd better get out and put the car in the carport right away. There's a steep slope up to it, and I was afraid I wouldn't be able to make it up the slope if there was very much snow on the ground. We hung up and I threw on my coat. I barely made it up the slope, it was snowing so hard. It didn't last long, though. When I got up this morning,

I thought I'd be completely snowed in, but there wasn't all that much; less than a foot."

"Yeah, I know. That storm went ripping right through! It'll be cold now for a few days."

"I can't never remember it being this cold." She looked around as if trying to remember where she was. "Well, I guess I'd better get home if you don't need me. Is there any other way out except through that room?"

Torgeson looked at Clay who shook his head. "I've still got to photograph those prints at the back door. I did the ones out by the road, and the ones out front, but I still want to look at the back some more."

"Sorry," Torgeson said gently to Mrs. Pettijohn. "I'll go out with you." Erica watched him impose his bulk between the woman and the sight of the blood-stained wall as he escorted her to the front door.

When he returned, Erica said firmly, "I still don't believe Herb killed Eugene. If there was only one set of tracks, and Eugene was killed last night, how did Herb get into the house to get the milk pail this morning?"

Clay leaned against the bedroom wall and pushed his hands into the pockets of the parka he was wearing over his uniform. "He probably took the pail with him last night and went out by way of the barn, so he wouldn't have to go back into the house in the morning to get it. There were two sets of his prints to and from the barn."

"Why would he want to milk the cow, anyway?"

"To feed his dogs maybe?" Clay shifted uncomfortably.

"He didn't know that he was going to need it until he got up this morning."

Torgeson pushed his pearl gray Stetson to the back of his head and rubbed his ears. "I ought to get myself a cap like yours," he said looking at Clay's wool-lined one with the ear flaps pulled down. "Damn, it's cold. Couldn't his dog have been sick last night, Erica, and he decided to wait till morning?"

"No."

"You're sure?"

"Of course I'm sure. I'm a vet, aren't I?"

"Sorry, Erica. I still keep thinking of you as Hugh Merrill's little girl."

Clay turned his back and sauntered over to the far side of the room to get out of range of the explosion. Erica controlled herself with difficulty, then with a tight-lipped hiss, she told Torgeson, "You might try calling me *Dr. Merrill* until you get used to the idea."

She picked up the cat carrier, brushed past the sheriff, pulled the door open, then turned back toward the two men. To Torgeson she said, "You haven't heard the last of me." And to Clay, "Don't worry. I wouldn't dare touch anything on my way out." She slammed the door behind her and made a haughty exit, stamping across the hardwood floor of the living room, yanking open the outside door and leaving it swinging. She answered the young deputy at the gate with a curt greeting that set him wondering what he'd done to deserve it.

"Hell," Torgeson snapped. "Now she'll go tell her daddy, and we'll have to answer to him."

CHAPTER 5

Back at her clinic, Erica put the Siamese into a cage on a soft blanket, gave her a litter pan and a bowl of water and pulled out Eugene Pettijohn's file.

"Can't remember what your name is, Puss. Something unusual, if I remember correctly." The cat's record revealed that her name was Aphrodite, she was six years old and had been spayed. "We'll have to think up another name for you," she said to the cat who cringed in a back corner of the cage. "You're an orphan now. Maybe we should call you Orphan Annie. I'll let you alone for a while to settle down. I'll come back and feed you later."

Mrs. Rushmore's cat, a huge, heavy-jowled tabby with a surly disposition, was in another cage. Erica had forgotten all about it. She went into the main part of the house and hearing her, Gram called out, "That you Erey?"

"It's me. Back at last." Erica began to pull off the heavy winter clothing.

"I took in Mrs. Rushmore's cat. I told her you were out on an emergency."

"Thanks Gram."

Clara Merrill, wearing an apron and wielding a rolling pin, looked up from her pie crusts. "I thought an apple pie might go over well in this weather, and there's a chicken in the oven roasting."

"Wonderful!" Erica kissed Gram on the cheek. "I'd starve without you."

"You probably would, at that," said Gram sternly, but there was a small smile of pleasure on her lined old face. "By the way, Mrs. Rushmore said Eugene Pettijohn had been murdered, shot I think she said. Is that true, do you know? One can't necessarily rely on what Mrs. Rushmore says."

"It's true." Erica fetched a mug from the cupboard and poured hot coffee from a large Thermos jug. There was always coffee on at Gram's place. "Someone shot him last night. I brought his cat back with me. The poor thing is absolutely petrified."

"The Siamese?"

Erica nodded.

"Maybe it would be more comfortable here in the house than in a cage."

"I'll go get her if you want."

"No, no. You stay there and drink your coffee. I'll finish this pie, then go get her. Do they know who shot Eugene?"

"They think they do, but I don't think they're right."

"Why not?"

"Herb Schultz discovered the body when he noticed that Eugene hadn't milked his cow and went to Eugene's house to see what was wrong. Herb was on his way down to Dibble's to call me, but he got Eugene's milk pail, went out and milked the cow, took the milk back to his pups, then went down to Dibble's and called me. He didn't report the murder until after he made sure I'd come out and take care of Queenie. Lyle Kline came out with the sheriff, and when he heard that Herb had milked a cow and fed his pups before he called the sheriff, he got all hot under the collar and claimed that only a guilty person would do that, so he took Herb in and is charging him with murder. That Kline doesn't know a cow from a billy goat. Everybody tried to explain to him that cows have to be milked when their udders are full, but he couldn't care less."

"Humph! I can't figure out why anyone voted for that city slicker, anyway. And him coming here from Boise just long enough to be able to get his name on the ballot! He just thinks of this town as a rung on the ladder he's trying to climb."

"The voters wanted change. Voters are fickle. Also, Otis had been county attorney for so long that probably half the populace felt he had done something to them or hadn't done something for them."

"That's ridiculous. We have never had a more competent or conscientious attorney."

"I know that, but people do stupid things."

"Surely Pete Torgeson will let Herb go if there is no more evidence against him than that."

"Unfortunately, it's not so simple. There is some other evidence, but I'm not sure it's conclusive either."

"I take it you don't think Herb shot him."

"No I don't. I think Kline's all wet, and I'm sure there's some other explanation for the evidence, which consists of tracks in the snow, but I think Kline is pulling some kind of strings and Pete Torgeson doesn't dare cross him."

"Why do you think that?"

"Because he's just doing whatever Kline says. He usually takes charge. I know that Otis let Pete gather the evidence in a case and didn't interfere, but Kline's trying to take charge of the investigation himself."

"Well, it's really not your concern. I expect they'll straighten it out."

"I don't know. Herb isn't my favorite person, but I can't believe he did anything other than what he says he did."

"He can be violent, though."

"Yeah. Barroom brawls, that kind of thing. But what they're saying he did is the work of a cunning liar. I just can't imagine Herb in that role."

Gram stood, her weight on one foot, hand on hip, and frowned as she thought. She sighed deeply and turned toward Erica. "I think, Erica, you'd probably better talk to your father."

That was the last thing Erica wanted to do. The comment about "Hugh Merrill's little girl" had stung badly. If she was going to stand on her own two feet, she couldn't go running to her Dad with every problem. She thought of Clay's obvious embarrassment at Torgeson's remark and wondered whether he'd had to put up with being known as "Darrel Caldwell's boy."

*   *   *

Darrel Caldwell's boy, however, had no qualms about going to his father to talk about the case. Clay Caldwell, when he went off duty that evening, drove out to his parents' farm, where his father had a roaring fire going in the machine shed in a stove made from a 55 gallon drum, and was engaged in his wintertime activity of thoroughly overhauling, cleaning and repairing his farm machinery. He usually kept his mind on his farming business, and when he did become involved in the political life of the community, it was because he had some very strong opinion on some specific problem. When that happened, he could become a tiger, and Hugh Merrill, a former county commissioner, had more than once been very happy to see Caldwell join the fray. The two men thought alike, and were invariably on the same side of the issue.

Darrel lay on his back on a creeper, underneath a tractor, preparing to drain the oil. Clay squatted beside the machine.

"This is the first time I've ever thought Pete was holding me back," the younger man said. "He seems afraid of Kline."

"Not of Kline. Of public opinion," came the muffled reply.

"What do you mean?"

"I mean, Kline just got elected by a sizable majority, only a short while ago. Pete Torgeson barely squeaked in. He's been in office for a long time and people get restless. Look at Vanderpool. The only thing that got Torgeson elected this time was that there are still a lot of people who remember his predecessor."

"You mean Cliff Bodine?"

"Yeah. Him."

"I don't know how he gets elected, even over in Salmon County. That guy is a total incompetent, besides which, he's a racist."

"Isn't he, though! Ever see the movie, *Casablanca*?"

"Twice. Why?"

"Do you remember that French chief of police who was always telling his cops to round up the usual suspects?"

Clay laughed at the memory.

"Well," the older man went on, "Cliff's just like that. His 'usual suspects' are all the Indians he can lay his hands on, and he just works on one or two of them until he forces a confession out of one by fair means or foul."

"I know. Pete won't loan me to him, but he's never asked anyway. Forensics isn't Cliff's thing."

"He says he doesn't need that fancy scientific stuff. He claims he gets results without."

"Don't I know it! But you know, he really doesn't get results. His statistics look good, because he 'clears' several cases whenever he gets someone to confess to something. Trouble is, the real crooks are still running free and doing more dirty work."

"Yeah, but it lets him brag to the citizens that he's getting results and that he's tough on crime and that's what people want to hear. What's the problem with this case, anyway?"

"Pete pulled me off it and set me to doing other things before I'd finished."

"Maybe he thinks you have all the evidence that's needed to convict this guy, Schultz."

Clay was silent for a minute, thinking. "Trouble is, I'm not sure that's right. There's a hitch somewhere, but I can't put my finger on it. So I want to keep working."

"And Torgeson won't let you."

"That's right. Don't get me wrong. I don't think Pete is doing it deliberately. I still think he's honest. But I think he's following Kline's lead too much."

"What do you want to do?"

"I want to investigate the case so thoroughly that if we go to court, there won't be any surprises, or if Schultz is guilty, I'm dead certain of it."

"Do you think he is?"

"I don't know. Probably."

"Who's his lawyer?"

"He doesn't have one yet. Kline's been yapping at him all day like a dog that sees a cat on the other side of the fence. Schultz just sits there and doesn't say anything."

"Has he been told he's entitled to a lawyer?"

"He has if Pete's been able to talk to him."

"I suppose he'll be stuck with the public defender."

"Yeah, but I haven't seen him around."

The older man pulled himself out from under the tractor, sat up and wiped his hands on a rag. "Clay, let me give you some advice. You went into law enforcement for the right reasons. Lots of guys don't. They want to be cops so they can pack guns and have power over other people. Don't get yourself screwed up. Think things through and do what you know is right."

Clay smiled at his father. "Thanks Dad."

"Now if you're going to stick around here, put on some coveralls and help me with this stuff."

*   *   *

Usually when Clay helped his father with the farm work, he could put his law enforcement job right out of his mind. He'd been helping his dad ever since he was old enough to pick up a tool. He had been taught by his dad, and knew exactly how, what and when to do things to help. They worked together silently as a perfect team.

Tonight, Clay couldn't keep his mind on what he was doing and occasionally Darrel Caldwell had to ask him for a tool or remind him of what needed to be done. Darrel understood, and didn't make an issue of it.

Clay kept thinking back to how he had been manipulated at every turn, by Kline, by the coroner, by the sheriff and by Erica. Her involvement bothered him. He was having enough trouble with the other law enforcement people he had to work with, and felt he could do without her tugging him in the opposite direction. She'd called him on the phone on the pretense of having to discuss the legalities of the care of Eugene's animals. He'd dropped by her clinic. As usual, he'd stayed to talk; he found he enjoyed being with her. The talk got around to the murder. She was still steaming, but willing to talk rationally. He had explained again the evidence of the footprints in the snow.

"Couldn't Herb have just walked in someone else's tracks? I do that when there are already tracks in deep snow and I don't want to be bothered making new ones."

"No," Clay explained. "I examined the tracks very closely. When I first went out there, I saw the one set of tracks up to the house and made sure I didn't disturb them. We knew from what Herb said over the phone that it was murder. That's why Pete sent me first. He knows I'll preserve the crime scene. He's tried to teach that to the others, but guys like Walt are set in their ways and don't learn real well. Walt worked under Cliff Bodine. He's the only one of Cliff's deputies that Pete kept on when he was elected, because Walt said he'd be loyal to Pete. He probably did it just to keep his job, but he's gone along with Pete's ways and never crossed him. But Walt still has a tendency to barge into things without thinking like they always used to do, and Pete doesn't always trust him not to destroy the evidence or give a suspect cause for complaint."

"Just how do you figure that there weren't any other tracks underneath?"

"Two ways. First, you could tell that Herb used a steady, even stride. You can't do that when you're trying to walk exactly in someone else's tracks. Also, if there had been other tracks made last night, they would have been frozen in place and when Herb walked over them this morning, he'd have knocked more snow into the tracks and his would have been visible as a second set. There was only one set going to the front door and one set leading out the back door to the barn."

"But Herb made those tracks this morning when he went to milk the cow."

"He *says* he made them this morning."

"But he did milk the cow."

"Yeah. He milked the cow all right. But he went into the barn from the road in order to do that."

"How do you figure that?"

"I think what must have happened is, Herb went in there late last night after it quit snowing. It had to be last night for everything to get that thoroughly frozen. Also it looked as if Eugene was still up in the evening. I don't know what time he usually goes to bed. I'll have to find out. Anyway, it didn't snow for very long. The snow came down real thick and fast, but when it quit, it quit! Also, the wind died right down. So Herb's tracks would still be perfectly preserved this morning.

"I think he must have gone in there, shot Eugene, then thought he could rig up a reason for having made tracks up to the house, by pretending he'd found Eugene in the morning and going out to milk the cow."

"But…"

Clay held up his hand to stop Erica's objection. "Herb must have gone into the kitchen after he shot Eugene, got the milk pail, went out the back door over to the barn and from the barn to the road. There were several sets of tracks to and from the barn, and those were all on top of each other so you couldn't tell just how many. The ones on top were Herb's, leading from the barn to the road. There were one or two headed the other way that weren't completely covered up, but it's like you said, he walked back and forth in the same tracks."

"You're sure they're all Herb's?"

"All the ones we can identify were made by the boots he was wearing this morning."

Erica pondered this information for a while, then looked Clay straight in the eye and said, "You're all wet!"

That stung and Clay flushed red. "How do you figure that?" he asked truculently.

"Stop for a minute and think about Herb. Forget about tracks. Do you think that Herb would have gone down there in the middle of the night to pick a fight with Eugene?"

Clay shrugged. "He might have."

"If he had taken a rifle with him, do you think Eugene would have let him in the house?"

"I don't know."

"Herb gets drunk on Saturday nights. If he went storming down to Eugene's with a hunting rifle and shot him, do you think he'd have the smarts to think up all that about the footprints? Herb isn't the brainiest person in the first place. I can imagine him having an argument and doing something violent, but the scene didn't look like that. It looked as if someone just walked in and surprised Eugene. Also, if Herb, in his drunken state, had killed Eugene, he'd have just floundered back out to the road and gone back to his house or maybe downtown to brag about it if he could find a ride. All this about covering up the fact that he had made prints in the snow is totally out of character for Herb, even when he's sober."

Clay was silent. Erica had put her finger on the weak area of the evidence. Lots of criminals are caught because they fit the profile of a person who would commit a crime in that particular way. Criminal profiling was out of Clay's element, but he could remember times when they had been confronted with a crime scene and known right off the bat who had done it by the way it was done. That was why the eldest Dibble boy, Luke, was now serving five years in the pen in Boise. The armed robbery he'd pulled off had his name all over it.

"What about the gun?" Erica asked. "Have you checked Herb's?"

"Yeah."

"Well, do you think it's the murder weapon?"

"We can't identify the weapon. The slug is too battered to get a match." Clay shrugged and looked miserable.

Erica, seeing her advantage, bored in. "When I was in Herb's house, I noticed that the living room was shut off, with a gunny sack under the door to keep the draft out. He hadn't gone in there for some time. The dust on the floor wasn't disturbed. Do you know whether Herb kept his gun in the kitchen?"

"He could have."

Erica caught the hesitation in Clay's voice. "But he didn't, did he?"

Clay hadn't been planning to tell Erica, but he'd been neatly caught. He sighed. "No. It was hanging on the rack in the living room. It didn't look as if he'd had it down since hunting season. He got his deer on opening day, and the gun didn't look as if it had been used since then. It was dusty inside and out." Clay paused a moment, then added. "He could have used another gun."

"Whose."

"I don't know yet. It could have been Eugene's own gun."

"Do you think he'd stop to clean it if he'd just shot Eugene with it? And how did he manage to get hold of it with Eugene standing right under the gun rack?"

"You ask too damn many questions."

Erica changed the subject. "Have you found Ronnie Bixby?"

"Yeah." There was obvious disgust in Clay's voice. "He was shacked up with Lolita Spillman in an empty house on the Spillman property."

"Lolita! I didn't think that girl would look twice at a kid like Ronnie. She likes them older, because kids Ronnie's age don't have any money."

"Well, she likes him well enough to marry him."

"What?"

"Yeah. They went to Marrying Sam last night and he claims to have married them. The little problem of a marriage license doesn't bother him. He tells them, after the service, and after he's collected his fee, that they have to go to the courthouse and get a license before it's official. Then they have to bring it back to him, and they do the paperwork after the fact."

Marrying Sam was a nickname given to a "preacher" who had a license as such from some place no one had ever heard of, and who married people, buried them, and occasionally ran fund-raisers for some unfortunate soul or other, keeping half the funds as his fee.

"Is Ronnie old enough to marry without his guardian's permission?" Erica asked.

"No, but things like that don't bother Marrying Sam."

Erica paused, her brown eyes thoughtful. "How did you know where to find them?"

"That was Walt. He figured they'd be there. He knows what all the dubious people in this county are likely to do."

"Oh? Then does *he* think Herb Schultz shot Eugene Pettijohn?"

*   *   *

Walt knew that Ronnie hung around Lolita Spillman. He went to Mabel's Tavern, where Lolita worked as a waitress and asked if anyone had seen Ronnie. Oh, sure, he'd been told. Ronnie had been mooning around the previous

51

evening at 10:30, when Lolita went off shift. Mabel's didn't serve food after 10, and the bartender and Mabel herself could deal with the booze after that time. Lolita usually gave Ronnie the cold shoulder, but last night she'd seemed interested in him and they had gone off together. They were looking very cozy. On a hunch, Walt went to Marrying Sam.

Around noon, Walt and Clay took the department's four-wheel-drive Blazer and drove up the Boulder Creek road to the Spillman property. A narrow road turned off and wound down the side of the canyon to a little flat beside a small creek. There was a fresh set of tire prints on the road. A car had gone down it, slipping and sliding, after the snow had fallen. Walt put the Blazer in four-wheel-drive and followed the tracks. Ronnie's old rattletrap was parked beside the vacant house.

"Don't know how they planned to get back out of here," Walt commented, kicking one of the threadbare tires.

Clay laughed. "I suppose they were so much in 'love', they didn't think ahead."

"Love, ha! They're just horny."

A wisp of smoke rose from the chimney, but there was otherwise no sign of life. Walt said, "You cover the back. I'll get them out of bed."

Walt pounded on the door with a heavy fist, then waited. There was no response. He pounded again and shouted, "Wake up in there. Police. We'll kick the door down if we have to." To add verisimilitude to this statement, he booted the door a couple of times.

"Wait a minute," a thin, reedy voice called out. "I'm coming."

"Make it snappy."

After a short pause, the door was opened by a slender youth with long, unkempt blond hair hanging down over his face. He had a faint stubble of beard on his chin and his gray eyes looked both tired and wary. He was hastily pulling on a pair of jeans and a sweatshirt and Walt could tell he hadn't bothered with his underwear. Walt pushed the door farther open and saw the girl, still in the makeshift bed on the floor beside the stove, the covers pulled up to her chin.

"What the hell do you want?" the youth blustered.

"We came to tell you that while you're out here fucking around, your uncle's been murdered."

At Walt's signal, Clay had come around to the door. He watched the youth's face turn pale and his body sway. Clay could have kicked Walt for his insensitivity. Ronnie got hold of himself, licked his lips, swallowed hard, and after a couple of unsuccessful efforts, managed to get a few words out.

"What do you want me to do?"

"Get dressed and come into town with us."

Ronnie turned and looked at the girl in the bed. She didn't look too pleased, but Clay couldn't tell whether her anger was directed at Ronnie, at the sheriff's deputies, or at the human race in general.

"What kind of shit-asses are you guys anyway, breaking in here on us like this? Why'd you tell anyone where we were going anyway Ronnie. Some honeymoon!"

"You ain't married yet," Walt told them. "After you get a proper license you can have yourselves another honeymoon. Come on, Ronnie. Get your clothes on proper. We'll watch while you do. Then you can come out to the Blazer with us and your girlfriend here can get dressed. Don't try anything cute. It's a long walk back to town, and it's real cold out there."

Lolita spat at Walt, who was well out of range, and Ronnie whined, "For cripe's sake, shut the door."

The two deputies stepped inside and watched Ronnie dress. They then escorted him out to the Blazer and waited for Lolita. Neither was dressed for the weather, and even in the warm interior of the vehicle, they shivered.

"Don't know how you two planned on getting out of here," Walt Forgey stated. "You slid down the road, but you'd never have made it back up in that car."

Clay, who was half turned in the passenger seat, saw Lolita give Ronnie a contemptuous look. This was more like Lolita. He wondered what had induced her to marry the youth.

An expert mountain driver, Walt took the steep road with just enough power to keep the momentum but not enough to spin the wheels, carefully keeping to the track they had made on the way down. The Blazer slowly climbed the quarter of a mile to the top. Clay felt his body tense and realized that he was holding his breath as they rounded a hairpin turn that would have left them stuck in a very awkward position if they hadn't made it. The Blazer came out of the turn smoothly and Walt eased it the last hundred yards onto the well-plowed rural road. Only then did Clay find his breath come easily.

When they arrived at the courthouse, which housed everything from the public health nurse's office to the jail, they turned the young couple over to Kline. It was then that Pete took Clay off the case and sent him to investigate an accident out on the river highway. He'd been busy with traffic until time to go off duty.

Fortunately, he'd gotten a lot of work done during the morning. The tracks in the snow up to Eugene's cabin had alerted him and he was more than normally aware of tracks for the rest of the day. There were Erica's tracks and Herb's footprints at Herb's shack. Across the road, he could see where Carl Nelson had driven into his lane while the snow was still falling, had gotten stuck in the dip, which had a frozen mud hole under the snow, and had walked on in to his trailer. A new set of footprints led out to the road and down to Eugene's house. Across the road from Eugene's, Lena Lemm had walked from her trailer and back twice. Clay had met both of them out by the road and asked whether they had heard a shot. Neither one had. He had questioned Jackie Dibble at length, but got nothing useful.

At the end of the day, Clay called his mother, who put some food into the oven to keep it warm for him, and drove out to the farm to talk to his father.

It was the first time Clay Caldwell had seriously questioned his choice of career.

CHAPTER 6

Lyle Kline surveyed himself in the mirror as he carefully knotted a flashy purple print tie. The voice of his wife, Jewel, floated out of the bathroom in its normal early morning whine.

"What do you intend to do about this murder case? It seems you haven't gotten very far with that old fart yet."

"Don't worry. I will."

"Well, I hope you have the trial pretty soon. I'm tired of living in this dump already. You'd better make it flashy so your name gets around and you can get a position in some place that's decent to live."

"Yes, dear." Kline smirked at his image in the mirror.

"You *will* win the goddam case, won't you?"

"Don't worry. I told the sheriff to keep working on him all night. He should be ready to cave in by now. I'll have a confession out of him before ten o'clock this morning."

Jewel wandered into the bedroom, leaned seductively against the door jamb and asked, "What good would a confession do? You don't want him to cop a plea, do you? You campaigned on the promise to take cases to trial, not to plea bargain. And that's the only way you'll get your name known."

"Relax." Kline shrugged into the coat of his slightly too bright blue suit. "You get a confession out of them, then they get to see a lawyer, probably the public defender, who is a complete idiot, and he tells the guy to retract his confession. So the case goes to trail, and I have this nice fat confession to wave in front of the jury."

"Okay, Mr. County Attorney." Jewel grasped the lapels of her husband's coat and pulled him toward her. She leaned down, as she was a good two inches taller than he and his built-up shoes were more than offset by her stiletto heels. She closed her eyes and parted her lips, and he dutifully succumbed. As they disentangled their various lips, tongues, arms and hands, she added, "Just get it over with in a hurry, will you. There's only one decent person to talk to in this whole burg and that's Marigold Considine, and her husband's a drip. I want to get back to civilization."

"We'll be out of here before the snow melts," he assured her.

*　*　*

Otis Vanderpool tripped with a light tread down the grand staircase of his sprawling house. Tall, lean and white-haired, he was still spry and proud of it. He ran everywhere in a sort of gangling lope. When he had been county attorney, courthouse regulars had become accustomed to him rushing about, leaning forward at a precarious angle as if constantly fighting a headwind. This morning he was clad in corduroy trousers, an old sweatshirt and moccasins, a sure sign that he intended to lounge around the house. In public, he dressed conservatively, always in suit and tie except when the temperature soared up over one hundred degrees, as it sometimes did in the summer. He also clung to the old-fashioned notion that the day should start with a hearty breakfast. He followed the aroma of frying bacon into the kitchen and took his place in the breakfast nook. His wife brought the coffee pot, poured a cupful for her husband and set the pot on a warmer nearby.

"I see old Herb Schultz finally went too far," she commented.

"What's that? What's he done?"

"The paper says he's been arrested for murdering a man named Pettijohn." Mrs. Vanderpool had learned years ago not to jump to the conclusions other folk did or risk a lecture from her husband. She would never have said, "Herb Schultz murdered Eugene Pettijohn," even though she might have thought so. Otis would immediately come to the defense of the person accused and present a ten-minute oration without knowing a single fact about the case in question. If Lyle Kline believed, as he had said in his campaign, that Otis Vanderpool didn't know how to try a case in court, it was because he had never bothered to observe. That so many defense lawyers had been eager to plea bargain when Otis had been the county attorney, was mainly because they knew his legendary prowess in the courtroom. Kline, to his peril, did not.

"Would that be Eugene Pettijohn," asked Otis, startled. "I hope not, or I'll have lost a good friend."

"I think so. I'll get the paper."

Otis scanned the front-page article in the Lincoln Morning Clarion. His steel-trap mind shifted into gear as he digested the details of the case, automatically cataloguing the errors in the coverage, the suppositions and innuendoes that were passed off as fact, and noting that all the quotes were from the cocky young lawyer who had beat him out. The sheriff was silent. To Otis Vanderpool, this meant one thing. The case was not nearly as open and shut as Lyle Kline made it out to be. He read and re-read, assimilating the material. Then with a sigh, he thrust the paper aside.

"Not my problem." His wife detected a wistful note in his voice. He turned his attention to the plate of bacon and eggs she had set before him, dismissing the murder case from his mind. He was leaning back in his chair, sipping his third cup of coffee (black — doctor's orders), when the phone rang. His wife answered it, but when he heard her say, "I'll go get him," he swigged the rest of his coffee and rose from the table.

"It's Darrel Caldwell," his wife said.

Hmm! Interesting! Darrel Caldwell wouldn't call with idle chatter. Must be something serious to make him call Otis at home this early in the morning.

"Hello, Darrel. How's the farm?"

"Oh, that's okay," Darrel Caldwell replied. "Look. I called you to suggest something you may not be interested in. But it could do you some good."

"Sounds interesting. What's the scoop?"

"You've heard about Eugene Pettijohn's murder?"

"I've just been reading all about it in the Clarion. The usual crap. I can tell they've got things all mixed up without knowing anything about it."

"Yes. Well, that's the Clarion! Then you know that Herb Schultz has been arrested for the murder."

"My old nemesis. Many is the time I've had him in the cells."

"I know. But always minor stuff, right?"

"That's right. Seems he's graduated, according to the Clarion. What has your son told you about the case?"

"Quite a bit. It's not nearly so cut and dried as the paper says."

"I figured that, since Pete Torgeson seems to have been very silent. What's your interest?"

"*My* interest is to ask *you* if you'd be interested in the case."

"Represent Schultz, do you mean?"

"Yeah."

"Not on your life! I've had too many run-ins with that old scoundrel. Also he hasn't a dime to his name. I'm picking and choosing my cases now, not working full-time. What I don't need are charity cases. Let the young guys who want to build up a reputation take them. I want to get paid. Do you know whether the public defender has been to see him?"

"No, I don't. But that wouldn't keep you from taking over would it?"

"It wouldn't, but I don't want to."

Darrel Caldwell's chuckle rumbled down the line. "Think again."

"What do you mean?"

"I mean that Kline beat you in the election by making the public think you couldn't try a case in court and that's why there are so many plea bargains. So, if you were to take on a high-profile case and beat the pants off Kline, it might do you a lot of good politically."

Otis was silent for a moment. Then he asked cautiously, "Do you know something about this case that isn't in the papers?"

"I know one thing. This murder is out of character for Schultz. No one would be surprised if he'd shot Pettijohn in a drunken rage. But this crime was done by someone who did a lot of planning and covering up. It's not like Schultz, drunk or sober."

"Hmm! I see what you mean. Good grounds for a defense. You mad at your son or something?"

"No. Why?"

"Just that if I defended Schultz and managed to get him off, it would make the sheriff's office look bad."

"Has it occurred to you that that's why they're not saying anything? Let Kline put his own foot in his mouth. Don't worry about Clay. Whatever he testifies to will be absolute fact."

"That doesn't mean I can't tie him in a knot."

"I'm not worried about Clay. He can take care of himself."

"Well, Darrel. It's an attractive proposition, all right. I won't promise I'll take the case, but I'll go talk to Schultz. He may not want me anywhere near him, but I'll trot down to the jail and see what gives."

"I *thought* you'd be interested."

"Thanks, Darrel."

Out on the farm, Darrel Caldwell hung up the phone and rubbed his hands in glee. "That'll make them sit up and take notice down there at the courthouse."

* * *

Lyle Kline took the elevator to the third floor of the courthouse, where the sheriff's office and jail were located, and went directly to the interview room. To his surprise, the room was empty. He swept through the room, out another door which led to the sheriff's office, banging his briefcase against the door jamb in his hurry. He passed through the outer office and into the sheriff's inner sanctum without acknowledging the formality of announcing his presence.

Pete Torgeson stood behind his desk, coffee mug in hand, poking through some papers. He looked up at the intruder, his brow creasing in annoyance. Kline threw his briefcase onto the sheriff's desk and in an accusatory tone demanded, "Where's Schultz?"

Torgeson made Kline wait while he took a long swallow from his mug. He set the mug down, composed his face into a bland expression, and replied, "In his cell."

"Oh. Has he confessed?"

"Nope. Hasn't said a word."

"He should be about ready to by now if you've done what I told you to and kept the pressure on all night. You have, haven't you?"

"Nope."

"What the hell have you been doing then? Get him down here."

"No."

"Get him down here!"

Torgeson's face hardened. He placed his bunched fists on his desk, leaned across it and stared down at the diminutive lawyer. "Let's get one thing straight, Kline. This is *my* jail and I'll run it *my* way. That way is the law of the land with regard to handling prisoners. In this jail, prisoners get to eat and sleep and go to the john. They also get to see their lawyers. The public defender said he'd be here first thing this morning. What he meant by 'first thing' remains to be seen. But I'm not going to lay myself open to charges of denying the prisoner his rights. He's just had breakfast. Next he gets to see his lawyer."

"That kid won't be here till the middle of the morning. I intend to go to work on Schultz in the meantime."

"No. We wait till they've had a chance to talk. Schultz isn't going to say anything to you, anyway."

"He would if you'd softened him up like I told you to."

Even the poker-faced sheriff couldn't keep the contempt off of his face or out of his voice. "No prisoner of mine is going to be subjected to either physical or mental cruelty."

"Well, you're just wasting time. Bring him in here!"

A third voice entered the conversation. Otis Vanderpool appeared at the door of the office, nodded to Torgeson and in tones dripping with suavity and good humor remarked, "I think I can solve your impasse. May I come in?"

"Of course, Otis. How are you?" the sheriff replied affably.

"What are you doing here?" Kline swung around to face the new arrival.

Otis Vanderpool strode into the office, found a chair, set his briefcase carefully beside it, hung his overcoat and hat in leisurely fashion upon the coat stand, sat down, crossed his long, elegantly clad legs and smoothed an imaginary wrinkle from his gray trousers. The sheriff could not suppress a grin. When Otis Vanderpool appeared in a three-piece suit, starched white shirt and sober striped tie, the clever attorney was about to spring some sort of trap. Pete Torgeson had worked with him long enough to know the symptoms.

"I have come to see my client."

They both stared at him in disbelief. The sheriff broke the silence. "Now, who would that be?" He knew the answer before he asked the question.

"Mr. Herbert Schultz. I understand you have arrested him and intend to charge him with the murder of Eugene Pettijohn. I request to be allowed to interview him before he is questioned any further. I further understand that to this point, Mr. Schultz has refused to make any statement except to deny having committed the murder. Is he aware of his rights?"

"He is." Torgeson couldn't help smiling. Kline resembled a boiler with a stuck safety valve, in imminent danger of exploding. His ears turned red, his cheeks puffed out and his eyes bulged.

Vanderpool clasped his hands in front of his chest, resting his elbows on the arms of the chair. His voice became pedantic. "May I remind you, Mr. Kline, that anyone who is accused of a crime is entitled to be represented through all stages of any proceeding involving him by an attorney."

"Don't try to tell me the law."

Vanderpool smiled indulgently.

"You must be hitting bottom if you're willing to take on a case like this," Kline spat.

"We'll see. We'll see."

"I'll have him brought in to the interview room," Torgeson offered.

"Oh, don't bother. I'll visit him in his cell, if you'll kindly grant me admittance to your inner sanctum." Vanderpool rose from his chair.

Kline's face showed the expression of someone about to throw up. *He* would never dream of going into the cell block.

*   *   *

The jailer slid back the outer door to the cell block to admit the lawyer. "Hi there, Otis. Long time no see."

"Hello Jerry. How are you doing? Has the wife recovered from her surgery?"

"She's fine. Just a bit tired now and then, is all."

"Good, good! Give her my regards."

"I'll do that. Now, who is to have the pleasure of your company?"

"Herb Schultz."

"Him? I don't think he'll consider it an honor."

Vanderpool laughed. "No. He probably won't, but if he's any sort of a gambler, he might see the value in having the man who always beat him on his side for once."

Jerry threw back his head and laughed. "You've got a point there!"

Herb Schultz lay on the cot in his cell, his ankles crossed, his hands beneath his head to supplement the skimpy pillow. His body, now clad in orange jail coveralls, was completely relaxed. He might have been a man resting in a hammock in his back yard. He didn't seem at all curious about the footsteps approaching along the corridor between the steel-barred cells.

"Hey, Herb. You got company," Jerry called out.

Herb rolled his head toward the sound of the jailer's voice, no expression showing on his relaxed features. Then his eyes focused on Vanderpool, he raised his head and looked again. Yep! That's who it was all right. He swung his feet to the floor and sat on the edge of the cot, his face settling into a truculent mask. Jerry unlocked the cell and the lawyer entered.

"I'll leave the door open. When you're through, just come back up front. Herb now, he ain't going nowhere. I don't hafta lock you in." Jerry disappeared back along the corridor.

"Hello, Herb."

"Yeah. What you want? I thought you was outta this business."

"I'm not the county attorney any more. I'm in private practice. I'm here to offer you my services. As a matter of fact, someone asked me to represent you."

"I don't need no lawyer. I didn't do it."

"Whether you did it or not doesn't matter. You need a lawyer. Now you can take me or you can take the public defender."

Herb scrutinized the lawyer through slitted lids, a surly scowl firmly in place. "I don't need no lawyer," he repeated.

"Yes you do. One will be appointed for you if you don't engage one yourself."

"That there's just so's you guys can make more money."

Vanderpool shook his head. "It is to ensure that anyone accused of a crime has legal representation through all phases of the process, from initial questioning through the trial and any appeals if necessary."

"Don't use all them big words. I don't know what yore talkin' about."

"What I'm saying is that you have the right to have a lawyer."

The scowl was gone, replaced by a crafty, sideways glance. "I cain't pay you."

"I know that."

Herb moved up toward the head of the bed and said to the lawyer, who was still standing. "Siddown."

Vanderpool sat on the foot of the cot, looking for all the world as if he had been offered a chair in an elegant drawing room. Herb observed him for several seconds. "What's in it for you?" he asked.

"Oh, lots of things."

Herb shifted his position. "You've put me in the slammer a lotta times."

"No hard feelings, I hope."

"Yeah, but I cain't just figger you out. Why should I hire you?"

"Because," Vanderpool replied quietly, "I can get you off."

Herb stared at him, frowning. The two sat in silence for several minutes, then the lawyer continued, "I always got you in when we were on the opposite side of the question. You'll have to admit that I'm effective. So who do you want? Me or the public defender?"

Herb's gaze dropped to the floor. "You, I guess," he mumbled.

"Okay, let's get down to brass tacks. What have you told the authorities?"

"I done told them I had nothin' to do with it. I just found him dead in the morning. They're makin' this big fuss over tracks. Well, I walked up to that house, so what. I left tracks."

"Why did you go up to the house?"

"To see what was wrong with Eugene."

"What made you think something was wrong?"

"'Cuz he ain't milked his cow, and then when I got down to his house, I saw the front door was open, which didn't seem right in this weather."

"How did you happen to notice the cow?"

"Well, it's like this. When I got up, I saw my dog was havin' fits. She done that the last time she had pups, too. So I knew she was havin' that there milk fever again. So I went down to Jess Dibble's to use his phone and call a vet, and when I was walkin' past the barn, I heard the cow and calf kickin' up a fuss. So I went in and took a look, and she ain't been milked."

Herb took several deep breaths as if the effort of such a long speech had exhausted him.

"Why didn't you go to Eugene's to phone? It was closer."

Herb snorted. "Me and him don't get along."

"Okay. Now what did you do after you went up to Eugene's cabin and found him dead?"

"I done got the milk pail and went out to the barn to milk the cow and feed her and turn the calf in with her."

"Then what did you do?"

"I done took the milk home and fed my pups."

"Then did you go phone?"

"Yeah. I went down to Dibble's."

"And phoned the sheriff?"

"Yeah. But I phoned the vet first. I told her to just go on up to the house and treat Queenie. That's my dog."

"Why didn't you phone the sheriff from Eugene's cabin when you found the body?"

"'Cause I had to milk the cow!" There was irritation in Herb's voice, as if he were trying to get a simple point across and no one would understand it.

"Was it Erica Merrill you called?"

"Yeah."

"Why didn't you call her from Eugene's?"

"Look, I didn't want to stay in that house with that stiff! I got outta there as quick as I could."

"You know that people think it strange that you did all these other things before you called the sheriff."

"Goddam it," Herb yelled. "I know that pipsqueak Kline don't know one end of a cow from the other, but the rest of you guys oughtta know."

"Take it easy. Yes, we do know that the cow had to be milked, but all this delay in reporting the murder doesn't look good."

"I don't know what the hell's the matter with you guys! Eugene was *dead.* He was so dead he was froze stiff. Whoever shot him coulda been a hunnert miles away already. He could wait. The ole cow and my dog couldn't. And onct I called the sheriff, I'd never of had time to do nothin' else."

"That sounds as if you knew you'd be arrested."

"It don't mean no such thing! I just knowed they'd take all day to figger everything out. My bitch woulda been dead."

"Okay, Herb. I get your point. Now, what did you do Saturday night? I know you were in the Deerhorn until ten or ten-thirty. What did you do after that?"

"I went home with Carl."

"And then?"

"I went to bed, goddam it."

"You didn't go down to Eugene's and have a quarrel with him?"

"Hell no! It was night. And it was cold enough to freeze the balls off a jackass."

"Were you drunk?"

"Shore, I was drunk. I always am on Sattiddy night. You oughtta know that."

Vanderpool smiled. Yes, he had lots of experience of that. Herb drunk was Herb quarrelsome. But would he have gone out of his way to pick a quarrel with his neighbor? Vanderpool rose.

"Okay, Herb. You'll be arraigned, probably today. I'll try to get you released on bail, but don't count on it."

"Don't bother 'bout that. I don't have no oil for my heater and it's warm in here. And the grub's not bad neither."

Vanderpool was chuckling as he walked along the corridor from the cell. But another thought was flicking through his mind. Erica Merrill — Clay Caldwell — Darrel Caldwell. The synapses in his fertile brain clicked shut completing the circuit. Darrel hadn't merely been calling to remind him of something for his own good. There was something else behind it. Something that had to do with the sheriff's forensic expert.

In the outer office, Pete Torgeson and Lyle Kline were still battling it out. Clay Caldwell, upon arriving on the scene, had skirted the field of battle and gone over to the coffee machine to collect a mug full of a liquid that most nearly resembled used crankcase oil. He took a tentative sip and screwed up his face as the taste hit home. Just then the door to the cell block opened and an apparition appeared. A tall, elegant, white-haired man stepped forth as if exiting his club. Clay's jaw dropped open.

Otis Vanderpool made a small bow in the direction of Lyle Kline and intoned, "Please inform me when the time of my client's arraignment has been set. By the way, we won't be asking for bail."

"You won't get it anyway," Kline snapped.

Vanderpool turned to the sheriff. "My client likes your jail. Good day." As he made his exit, he bumped into a gangly young man whose joints seemed insecurely put together, and who was rushing into the office.

"Oops. Sorry," he called after Vanderpool, then turned to the people in the office. "Hi. I guess I'm supposed to take this murder case. Can I see the guy?"

"You're too late," said the sheriff. "His attorney just walked out the door."

Clay Caldwell choked on the mouthful of coffee he had been swallowing.

CHAPTER 7

The sheriff's secretary, dispatcher and general dogsbody, could hardly wait to spread the news. At the first opportunity to leave the sheriff's office, she traipsed down the stairs to the second floor where the assessor's office was located. There, she told the clerk, "Otis Vanderpool came in this morning, dressed fit to kill, and said he's going to represent Herb Schultz in our murder case."

"Really! Somebody must be paying him."

"Well, I know that Merrill girl thinks Herb is innocent. And the Merrills have lots of money."

As soon as the sheriff's secretary had gone back to her eyrie on the third floor, the assessor's clerk hustled down the stairs to the main floor, where she found the secretary to the County Commissioners, walking along the corridor.

"Guess what I just heard."

The secretary stopped in her tracks. "What?" she asked, her voice eager with the anticipation of juicy gossip.

"Otis Vanderpool is going to represent Herb Schultz and there's probably Merrill money behind it. That Merrill girl, you know, the vet, thinks Herb didn't do it."

"Oh, really!

This exchange was heard by a housewife who was trudging up the stairs to report for jury duty. As soon as she entered the courtroom where the jury panel was marshaling, she sought out another woman and reported, "I heard some officials talking while I was coming up the stairs. They said that new vet, Erica Merrill, has hired old Vanderpool to be Herb Schultz' lawyer in that murder."

"Erica? She don't have no money. I bet its her Dad what's footin' the bill."

The two women were not among those chosen for the jury of the day, so by noon, the gossip had rippled out to lap upon all the shores of the town.

*　　*　　*

Blissfully ignorant of the "news" swirling about, Erica began another day at the office. Ignoring the cold, a client with a cat to be spayed dutifully delivered it promptly at eight o'clock. Kelly, Erica's assistant, took the squirming cat, tucked her expertly under her left arm while pulling out the client's file.

"Boy, did she want her breakfast this morning," said the client. "I usually feed her at six and she couldn't figure out why I wouldn't give her anything this morning."

Kelly smiled and commiserated with the client, rattled off the request to pick up the patient between four and five that afternoon, and handed out a sheet of post-surgery instructions.

Erica examined the sleek, healthy young calico, then gave her the pre-surgery tranquilizer, pain-killer and atropine. Kelly popped her into a cage, and while she set out the surgery packs, uncovered the anesthesia machine and placed a clean pad on the surgery table, she plied Erica with questions about the murder.

"How come you were out at Eugene's when they found his body?"

"I wasn't. I had to go to Herb Schultz's to treat Queenie. She had eclampsia again. I wish he'd get that dog spayed. It would save him money in the long run. It would be cheaper than constantly getting me out on emergency calls."

"Did he pay you?" Kelly asked in astonishment.

"No. I entered everything in the computer, by the way."

"If he didn't pay you, he won't. I know from working for George before you came. He never paid George, either. So it doesn't matter how much you *charge* if he doesn't ever pay it anyway." Kelly was nothing if not practical. "So how'd you get in on this murder?"

"Herb found Eugene's body. He was down at Eugene's cabin while the sheriff was investigating, so I went to talk to him. That's when I found out he was being arrested."

"But you don't think he did it?"

"I don't really know. But the reason that new county attorney, Kline, gave was idiotic. I can't stand Kline. So I challenged him."

"What did he think of that?'

"He told me to get lost." Erica smiled when she recalled the scene. None of the law enforcement officers, she felt, had dared to challenge Kline, so she had done so. She knew the others had understood her, probably felt the same themselves, but didn't seem to have the guts to stand up to him. Well, she did!

They took the calico cat from its cage and zipped her into a bag made of rip-stop nylon — a contrivance that had saved them many a battle scar. Only the cat's head stuck out, and over this they placed the anesthesia mask. When she had relaxed into unconsciousness, they rolled her out of the bag, and inserted an intra-tracheal tube, which they attached to a hose from the anesthesia machine. While Erica scrubbed, Kelly prepped the patient. As Kelly helped Erica into a sterile gown, she asked, "If you don't think Herb killed Eugene, who do you think did?"

"I haven't the foggiest. Maybe Herb did do it. I merely wanted to put a flea in Kline's ear. Now, let's not talk about it while we're doing surgery. Let's concentrate on what we're doing."

The heart monitor beeped its regular rhythm as Erica made an incision, removed the ovaries and uterus, and closed the abdomen.

"George does it differently," Kelly commented.

"He probably does. I've picked up ideas at surgery seminars I've gone to."

"So George does it wrong, then."

"No, no! Not wrong. Just differently."

"Then you mean there's more than one way to do things."

"Exactly. No one person's way is right where others are wrong. It's a matter of personal preference."

"Oh! I thought they taught you to do everything alike.

"In a way, they do. I can look at an incision and tell whether the person who did the surgery learned it at WSU or somewhere else. People tend to stick to the way they were taught. But I've picked up new ideas here and there. Whenever I see something I like, I use it."

"I see."

A few minutes after being put back in her cage, the cat raised her head and shakily viewed a topsy-turvey, anesthetic-skewed scene of cage bars and of people staring intently at her. She sighed, decided to give it up for a while, and lay her head down to sleep.

"She looks like Herb Schultz on Saturday night," Kelly commented.

"She does. That's exactly why I don't think Herb killed Eugene. I think he did what this cat is doing. He went to bed to sleep it off."

The remainder of the morning brought an odd assortment of canine and feline problems. No one mentioned the murder. At eleven thirty, the phone rang. Kelly answered it and listened to a torrent of words, finally saying, "Okay, I'll tell her."

"What was that about?"

"Mrs. Glaser canceled her appointment for this afternoon."

"She did a lot of talking. Did she say why she canceled?"

"Yeah."

"Well, what was it?"

Kelly shifted her weight nervously and looked away. "She said she didn't want to have anything to do with someone who associated with low-life scum like Herb Schultz."

"Herb had a sick dog that has just as much right to medical care as Pierre," Erica grumbled, referring to Mrs. Glaser's Miniature Poodle.

"She didn't mean that. She said you're paying for Herb Schultz's lawyer."

"*What!*"

"Are you?"

"Of course not. Mrs. Glaser is all screwed up, as usual."

Kelly shrugged. "Well, it's none of my business, but I'd never give that old goat the time of day."

"Who are you calling an old goat—Herb or Mrs. Glaser?"

"Why, Herb of course."

"It could apply to either of them."

Kelly tittered.

By noon, the spayed calico was on her feet, restlessly pacing the cage, yowling for food. Erica called the owner and told her she could pick up her cat at one o'clock. She locked the office door and went upstairs to lunch. She was digging into a bowl of Gram's beef stew when they heard the bell on the clinic door ring. Gram frowned. "I suppose you'd better answer it. I'll pop your stew into a warm oven to keep it hot for you."

"There's a sign by the clinic door that says, 'Hours — 8 to 12 and 1 to 5. They can read it and come back later." Erica took a large bite of cornbread.

"What if it's an emergency?"

"Gram. I'm eating! If it's an emergency, they'll come to the front door."

Which was exactly what the client did. It was no emergency, however, but Mrs. Rushmore to pick up her cat. With poor grace, Erica led her downstairs and got the carrier. "You'll have to take him out of the cage. He doesn't like us." To give emphasis to this statement, the fat-jowled tabby let out a venomous hiss.

"I don't know what you people do to him. He's *such* a sweet cat," Mrs. R complained.

"We don't do anything to him. We don't even touch him. We put his food and water and his litter pan in the front of his cage so we can change them without handling him."

Erica opened the cage. Mrs. Rushmore reached in to get the cat, dragging him across the dishes in the front of the cage and knocking the litter pan and water dish onto the floor. Of course, the cat had just minutes before emptied his bowels, the stinking residue of the low-quality canned food he normally ate splatting onto the tile floor amid showers of kitty litter and water. Mrs. R stepped hastily back, wrinkling her nose as she regarded the mess, obviously blaming Erica for the unpleasantness. She clutched the cat to her bosom, rubbed her face in his fur and crooned, "My poor Bootsie. Did ums miss his mommy? Mommy will take you home, away from this awful place."

Erica bit back an angry retort.

With the cat in its carrier, Mrs. R stopped at the front desk to pay the bill. Erica quoted the fee, resisting the temptation to multiply it by a hundred. Mrs. R, as usual, complained. At least she didn't kiss her money good-bye as one client was wont to do. Instead, she took the proffered receipt, folded it and put it in her purse.

"I won't be back, you know."

Good! Erica thought, but aloud she asked, "Why?"

"Because I don't think much of anybody who'd stick up for that old bum, Herb Schultz. That man's dangerous,"

Mrs. R spat maliciously, looking for all the world like Boots, her cat.

"He may not be a nice man, but that doesn't mean he killed Eugene."

"Of course he did!"

"How do you know?"

"Well, the police say so."

Erica sighed in annoyance. "I liked Eugene. I want to see his murderer caught. But I want to see the *right* person caught. I don't know for sure, but I doubt that it was Herb Schultz. The sheriff's office also has doubts, I think."

"They arrested him, didn't they?"

"On orders from the county attorney. But I expect that when they finish their investigation, they'll let him go."

"Hmmph!" Mrs. R marched out.

That afternoon, one client called to cancel, giving no reason. Two others failed to keep their appointments. Erica let Kelly go home early. She read her veterinary journals until boredom became so thick she could hardly turn the pages. She cleaned her desk. She talked to the calico, who didn't go home until nearly five after all. She tried to find other things to do.

She called the client whose dog was scheduled for neutering the next day.

"Oh! We can't come."

"Why not?" Erica asked.

The client floundered around trying to think up an excuse, finally saying that her kids were sick. *Likely story*, Erica thought.

At five, she locked the door and went upstairs. Her father was there, waiting for her.

"Erica, I'd like to have a word with you."

Gram, who had been talking to her son, got up and discretely left the room.

"Okay." Erica flopped into a chair and regarded her father inquiringly.

Hugh Merrill cleared his throat. "Erica, have you hired Otis Vanderpool?"

Erica raised her eyebrows and stared at her father in mock surprise. "No. But I would if I needed a lawyer. I think he's a good one."

"He is. But that's not what I mean."

"Well, what *do* you mean then?"

"I have been told that you hired Otis Vanderpool to represent Herb Schultz in this murder case. I have been told furthermore that you expect me to pay for it."

The last was a real surprise to Erica, though by now, the first part was not.

"Who told you that?"

"Who told me is of no consequence," her father replied sternly. "The news is all over town."

"*Who* told you?"

Hugh Merrill eyed his daughter, whose dark-eyed gaze impaled him like a skewer. "The chief of police."

"And where did *he* get this news."

"Probably from the sheriff's office. They occasionally do speak to each other, even if the city police won't let the sheriff use their radio frequency and won't listen to the sheriff's, so they can't communicate with one another."

"I seriously doubt if it came from Pete Torgeson. He's an honorable man. He wouldn't tell lies. Besides, I don't think he'd give out information like that even if he knew it."

"Are you saying you didn't hire Otis?"

"I didn't hire Otis. I didn't hire any other lawyer. And I wish my own father had more faith in me. If I'd hired anyone, I'd pay for it myself."

"But you don't have any money."

"Then I'd have to consider that if I wanted to hire a lawyer, wouldn't I. Look, Dad, I appreciate the fact that you've loaned me money to start this practice, but otherwise,

I intend to make my own way. I'm not going to come running to you every time I want something."

"Fair enough. But you still haven't answered my first question."

"What question?"

"Did you hire Otis Vanderpool?"

"I thought I'd answered that quite clearly. I did not hire Otis or any other lawyer."

Hugh sighed and glanced away. "Then we've got to do something about the gossip."

"What?"

"I don't know."

"What's wrong with both of us just denying it?"

"Look, Erica, I've spent most of my life trying to build up a good reputation in this county. I'd appreciate it if you would consult me before you did anything to damage it."

"I just told you I didn't do it," Erica shouted. "Can't you hear?"

"It's not just about Otis. It's about your taking sides with Herb Schultz against the sheriff and the county attorney and making a spectacle of yourself where you shouldn't even have been butting in."

"I did not butt in. I did not make a spectacle of myself. And if I don't think Herb Schultz killed Eugene Pettijohn, that's my own damn business." Erica hoisted herself out of her chair and flounced out of the room, down the stairs to her clinic and into her office, slamming the door behind her.

Damn! Hell! What had she done to deserve this?

She picked up the phone and dialed Clay's home number, bent on passing on the vinegar and gall. She let it ring eight times before she hung up and tried the sheriff's office.

"He went to Lincoln. He isn't back yet," the dispatcher informed her. "Do you want him to call you?"

"Never mind." Erica slammed the receiver into its cradle.

Gram called down the stairway that dinner was ready. Erica's churning stomach was in no condition to accept food. She'd pass up supper tonight, especially if her dad was staying, which he probably was. She wished it wasn't so cold. A good fast walk down the path by the creek would have done a lot of good. She sat and brooded, going over and over the perceived insults and slights she had received. When was anyone going to accept her in her own right?

There had been animosity between farmers and loggers ever since Merrills had homesteaded here. Environmentalists had been warring with loggers for years. It would probably take just as long for the population of this town to accept a woman vet. Not an encouraging prospect.

At about eight o'clock her phone rang. It was Clay.

"I just got back from Lincoln. God, what cold weather to drive in. My feet are frozen."

"What were you doing in Lincoln?"

"Forensic stuff. Say, I heard it was you who hired Otis to defend Herb Schultz. You didn't, did you?"

"I did not!"

"Good, I'm glad to get that cleared up. I nearly swallowed my Adam's apple when I saw him walking out of the cells this morning. You should have seen the expression on Kline's face."

Erica laughed, much of the tension draining away.

Then Clay said, "Hey, you'd better be careful, Erica. It's all over town that you're claiming that Herb is innocent. I have a hard time defending you and myself at the same time. You're making Pete and me look bad."

"I had no intention of making you look bad. It was Kline who was making an ass of himself."

"Well, we have to work with him, so don't rock the boat."

"I'm *sorry* that I should have an opinion of my own," Erica snarled and slammed the receiver back into its cradle.

Damn! No one believed her. No one respected her. Her practice was going to hell. There seemed only one course of action for her to take. She'd go out and solve the damned case herself!

CHAPTER 8

After Otis Vanderpool left the jail and he got rid of Lyle Kline, Pete Torgeson called Clay into his office.

"Look here, Clay, having Otis enter the picture changes things. I was willing to go along and see if Kline could get a confession out of Herb, but that won't be any good when we're up against Otis. We have to have an iron-clad case."

Clay nodded.

Torgeson went on, "So I'm putting you on it full time. Don't leave anything to chance. What do you still have to do?"

'I've been working up the diagrams of the room and of the exterior of the house and barn. I got all the measurements yesterday. I'd like to go over Eugene's whole house. I'd also like to do Herb's place."

"Okay, go ahead."

"Is it okay to build a fire in Herb's shack? It'll be pretty damn cold to do a thorough search otherwise."

"I don't see what harm that could do. You left the electric heat on at Eugene's, didn't you?"

"Yes, I did."

"Anything else? There isn't any point in looking at people's guns, I don't suppose."

"No. The only thing would be to see if one had been fired recently, but everyone out here has a legitimate reason for shooting a rifle. I can do one thing with the slug, though."

"What's that?"

81

"I could take it down to Lincoln Ammo and see if it's one they manufactured."

"Could they tell that?"

"Sure. They'd take a little scraping of metal and do a spectrographic analysis. Every manufacturer's is different. Also, the copper jacket varies from one manufacturer to another."

"So what if it is one of theirs?"

"Then that doesn't tell us much because nearly everyone around here uses their product. But if it isn't theirs, they might be able to tell who made it. If we were really in luck, it might be a hand loader. I only know of two of them around here."

"Hmm. Worth a try, I guess. Okay, after you've done the other stuff, take a car and go down to Lincoln. You might as well take those rolls of film for development while you're at it."

So Clay went back to his favorite work, his heart singing, thanking his lucky stars that Otis Vanderpool had gotten in on the case. Clay would rather pit his considerable talents against the wiles of the old lawyer than to tell cautious half-truths to that bumbling young public defender. He did not know how Vanderpool had entered the case and his brain did not register the same line of cause and effect that Vanderpool's had. The synapses stayed open.

In Lincoln, he dropped the film off at a commercial establishment whose owner did photography work for the Lincoln police. "This is police stuff," Clay explained, pushing a work order across the counter.

"Your murder?"

"Yeah."

"Okay. I'll do all the work myself. Come back in an hour." He grinned. "Absolute confidentiality guaranteed."

Clay had called in advance to the office of Lincoln Ammunition, Inc. and a technician was waiting for him. He watched while the man did his work. On a previous occasion he had been given a tour of the plant, which was built so that if there was an explosion, it would literally raise the roof. The roof was not fastened to the walls, but rested on supports. It was designed so that the force of an explosion in the plant would be expended upward, the roof raising off its supports, rather than outward, causing walls to crumble. Since the force of an explosion would be harmlessly dissipated, injury to personnel would be minimized. They had never had the opportunity to test the design in actual practice, for which they were thankful.

They had never experienced an explosion in the old plant, which preceded this one, either, but Clay knew a man who had learned about the explosive power of gunpowder the hard way. This man worked at Lincoln Ammo in the old days, when the floor was covered with a layer of water and the employees were told to keep their boots greased and never let them dry out. The man went on a holiday and when he returned, he disregarded the instructions and put on his now dry boots in preparation for going back to work. Walking along, he had scraped one boot against the other, starting a conflagration which burned his boots and seriously burned his feet, but left his Levi's, those heavy denim blue jeans, untouched. Frantically looking for a water hose, he had found a puddle and desperately doused his burning boots. He spent six weeks in the hospital before he could hobble around again.

Clay collected the report, gathered up the finished pictures, and locking his evidence carefully in the official car, went to his favorite steak house for a thick, juicy T-bone before heading back upriver.

He stopped at Pete Torgeson's house to show the sheriff the results of his day's work before going to the courthouse to turn in the car and lock away the evidence.

Torgeson shuffled through the pictures, noting especially the clear, crisp photos of the tracks in the snow. He handed them back. "Okay, what about the slug."

"It's a thirty-thirty. Part of a batch they made in August of this year; hundreds of thousands of rounds. They

83

hit the stores in the early fall, before hunting season. Everyone in this neck of the woods had a legitimate right to own some."

Torgeson groaned. "I guess that's all we could expect."

"Yeah."

"So the gun that fired it could be any gun in the county—or out of it for that matter — and the ammo could have been in anyone's home."

"Any but one," Clay corrected him.

"How's that?"

"Any but Eugene Pettijohn's."

Torgeson frowned at his deputy. "How do you figure that?"

"Eugene had an open box of Remingtons in the drawer of his desk with just three shells missing. Furthermore, his are the only prints on the handle of that drawer."

"But he could have had a box of Lincolns also."

"I don't think so. He was a very methodical man. The guy down at the gun shop said he always bought Remingtons. He thought that the last time was in the summer when Eugene wanted to give Ronnie some lessons. Also, Eugene wouldn't open a new box until he'd used up the old. If he had a few from one box sitting around, he wouldn't have opened up another box to get out just three shells. Lots of guys would have, but not Eugene."

The sheriff grunted. "You know, this is the first case I ever remember having to go over the habits of the *victim* so damn thoroughly. The suspect, yes. You're always doing that, but the victim is usually just some dead guy. It's usually pretty obvious who he is, what he's been up to, and why the suspect knocked him off. This here's a different sort of case."

"Yes, but we still have to do the same sort of thing with the suspect in this case. And that's going to be harder."

Torgeson scratched his head. "And don't think old Wily E. Coyote, Otis Vanderpool won't let us know that!"

*   *   *

After Clay left the photos and reports at the sheriff's office, he slogged through the snow to his pickup truck, hoping it would start. The engine turned over a couple of times, complaining about being made to work in such bitter cold. Then it caught, and after a wheezy cough, roared into life. Clay let it idle until it was running smoothly, then eased out onto the ice-slickened street and headed for the coffee shop. He lived in a rented room and usually ate out. No longer hungry, but feeling the chill of the long drive up the river, he sought the cheerful warmth of the café.

As he eased his frame into a booth, he noted a group of men sitting in the largest of the booths at the back of the café. He hoped they wouldn't notice him. He was not popular with them, and he did not like them much. One, a non-stop loud-mouth, was in full cry. Clay could not help overhearing. The gist of the torrent of words seemed to be that Eugene Pettijohn was no loss to the community, but that Herb Schultz would not be either, if he were executed or put away for life. The cashier, who shared waitress duties with another woman, wandered down to that end of the cafe, listening to the customer's oration. She found a chance to squeeze into the conversation while the man drained his coffee cup.

"Yeah, I agree," she said. "But that Merrill girl oughta be careful. If she don't look out, she won't have no more clients. Why, my sister told me she canceled her appointment with Erica this afternoon, cuz she doesn't want anybody to think she approves of what that girl's doing. 'Specially her old man — him having had a fight with Herb one time, so he might get mad at her if she took Herb's side."

"Yeah, that's right," said the loud-mouth. "I've heard other people say they'd be embarrassed to be around her. It won't do her business no good, scaring people away. Besides, she's away too much. My brother's ex-wife's neighbor went over there about six-thirty last night after she'd had supper and Erica was gone off somewhere."

"I hear she's a good vet, though," the cashier reflected.

"Is she? How the hell can you tell? I'd pick one by what they charge. They all charge too damn much, though. You can't afford to go to them. Besides, my brother-in-law has a neighbor who can do all that stuff. He buys the shots for his dogs from some big outfit, and he can fix cats a whole lot cheaper than those vets do. He only charged me ten bucks. I took my cat out to his place last week to get it fixed, and he just shoved him in a boot and cut off his balls. Only trouble is, there was blood all over the seat of the car, and when we got home, that cat ran lickety-split under the house and I ain't seen it since. I guess he'll come out when he gets hungry enough."

"If he hasn't bled to death. That happened to one of mine when I tried to do it myself," another man chimed in.

"So what the hell! There's more cats. But I don't think a woman should be a vet in the first place. It's not fit stuff for a girl to do and it takes jobs away from guys who need them so's they can feed their families. She oughta marry that there other vet and let him do the work while she raises a family."

"She's nice though," said the cashier.

"Yeah, I guess she's nice. None of them Merrills puts on airs anyway."

Another man in the group spotted Clay and detached himself from the group in the back booth. He came over and slid in across from Clay. Clay recognized him as a former deputy, one of Cliff Bodine's men, one who Torgeson hadn't kept on. He was a lean man, with short-cut white hair and a red scar from cheek to chin. He claimed that the scar came from a knife fight with an Indian, but Clay knew that he'd gotten it in a drunk-driving accident that had been hushed up back in the old sheriff's day.

"Hi, Clay. I guess you got yourself a nice murder case."

"Murder is never nice," Clay replied acidly. The other man paid no attention to the remark.

"You think Herb Schultz did it?"

Clay shrugged. "Seems like the best suspect to date."

"There's a lotta guys who think he oughtta get a medal or something. Eugene Pettijohn ain't no great loss."

Clay's face flushed. "I don't happen to agree with you."

"Anyway, what I came over to tell you is that if you're still looking around for someone else, I know where you might look."

"Oh yeah! Where's that?"

"Well, early Saturday evening that kid that lived with Eugene was strutting around town with his thirty-thirty Winchester."

"We knew that."

"He wasn't alone."

"No. I don't suppose he was."

"Those two kids he always hangs out with were there, and guess who else?"

Clay didn't answer right away and the man sat there with an eager expression, dying to spill his guts. Clay easily identified "those two kids" as young troublemakers the town police and the sheriff alike kept a watchful eye on. The man went on, "One of them Injun kids, that's who. And you know what they're like. Can't trust 'em as far as you can throw a Brahma bull by the tail. I betcha they could of gone up to Eugene's and shot him."

"I find most of them quite trustworthy, *and* law-abiding."

"Wait till you've been in the business a few years longer, then you'll see."

"Go away and leave me alone. I'm off duty and I want to relax and have a cup of coffee."

"I just thought you'd like to know that the Injun kid was Charlie Oliver."

That jolted Clay, and as the man slid out of the booth and ambled back to the group, he tried not to let it show.

Charlie was the younger brother and spitting image of Louie Oliver, with whom Clay had toiled through a grueling but wildly exciting season of high school football in the black and gold colors of the Boulder Yellowjackets. As a sophomore, Clay who had been large for his age and unusually well-coordinated, had made the all-league team at center. Behind him were Wade Merrill, the all-state quarterback, and two running backs who also made the league all-star team. Bill Clarke was the big pounding fullback who got the tough yardage, and Louie Oliver, a full-blooded Indian boy, had been the tailback, possessed of slippery moves and agile Mercury-winged feet. They had swept all their games, an irresistible force on offense. In one game, they had scored seventy points, Louie Oliver getting twenty-four of them. They had even beaten Lincoln High in an exhibition game, though Lincoln had four times as many students. They had advanced to the finals of the state tournament for schools of their size, and in the domed stadium at the University of Idaho, wearing the same colors as the Idaho team which they idolized, they had beat the pants off the defending four-time champion.

Early in the season, the papers had noticed the team's success, but the thing that caught the fancy of the media was the names of the two backs. This is Lewis and Clark country. Two hundred years after those intrepid explorers had passed this way, they are still commemorated in parks, historical sites, and names. Everything, it seems, is named after Lewis and Clark.

So Louie became Louis, and Boulder's backfield boasted Louis and Clarke. The media rolled in it like a feline in catnip.

Even at that, football was not Louie Oliver's best sport. He lived for basketball. His exploits on the hardwood were even more impressive than those on the turf.

All the boys except Clay were seniors that year, and Boulder's success was not repeated. Coach Stew Kinch retired after that glorious season, ending a twenty-two-year career at Boulder High. He still lived in town, tending his roses and making observations for the weather bureau in Lincoln. He had been Clay's science teacher as well.

Louie had gotten his diploma, standing proudly in his cap and gown, grinning from ear to ear. He'd gone on to play with the all-Indian basketball team at Forks, the Indian reservation headquarters, but his career was cut short by a tragic injury to his father.

Jackson Oliver was an old-time rodeo cowboy, and Clay could remember him winning the saddle bronc riding at the Lincoln Stampede. He had a stable where he broke and trained horses. Louie helped him when he wasn't off at a basketball tournament. Then one day, a young horse had reared and fallen over backward with Jackson, who had tried to scramble out of the way. But he couldn't get free and the cantle of the saddle had come down across his back, leaving him a paraplegic. Louie had come home to take over the business. Jackson was barely out of the hospital when his wife caught pneumonia and died. Louie effectively became the head of the family. His teen-age sister dropped out of school to do the housework, nurse her father, and care for the younger boy, Charlie.

Jackson found that he had the Indian's knack for hand-made crafts. He taught himself to make jewelry of silver, inlaid with turquoise and jade. His work was sold on consignment at a gift shop down on the highway. He eked out a meager existence from this work.

So Charlie spent his formative years in a household headed by a boy barely out of high school and a teen-aged girl. He began to drift aimlessly. The only thing that kept him in school was basketball. Clay was very much afraid that

Charlie might slide into a life of idleness, and possibly petty crime. So far he had not.

Clay realized that, not only was he worried about Charlie Oliver, he'd been extremely upset by the opinions of the people in the cafe about Erica. Did she really mean that much to him? Yes, he decided, she did. They'd been very close in high school, dating steadily throughout their senior year. And there had been that one time... He didn't want to see her hurt, and was resentful of her detractors.

Soberly he made his way home, wanting someone to talk to. He called Erica — and had the phone slammed in his ear.

CHAPTER 9

In the half-light of early morning, Erica turned her Cherokee into the Dibble driveway (neatly plowed by the county snowplow) and parked by the rambling house. Country people were always up early and would think nothing of her dropping by at seven to check on Queenie.

The clear sky overhead glowed a faint blue and the stars gradually winked out, but the house was ablaze with light. Set in a clearing among the pines, it had been added onto every now and then as the family had grown, and now rambled this way and that in a hodgepodge of architectural styles. The latest addition had been a huge kitchen, big enough for the whole family to do everything but sleep in. Smoke curled from the black stovepipe rising from the kitchen roof, rose a few feet and spread out in the still air, seeping between the trees.

As Erica got out of her vehicle, she inhaled a great lungful of air, redolent of pine and of wood smoke. She instantly fell into a fit of coughing as the stinging cold penetrated deep into her lungs.

Jackie Dibble stood in the doorway, having seen the approaching headlights. "Oh, it's the Doc! Come on in. You'll catch your death of cold out there. Come to see Queenie? Well, you're just in time for breakfast, so take off your coat and pull up a chair."

"How is Queenie?" Erica asked when she could find a crack in the torrent of words.

"She's fine. She hasn't had no more fits, or seizures or whatever you call them. The pups is sure growing. Eddie Lee, come tell the Doc about your pups." The last sentence was bellowed in a voice that sent reverberations through the rafters.

The nine-year-old boy ran into the room, still wriggling into a sweatshirt with a Seattle Seahawks logo. He scooted over to the box beside the stove where Queenie and family were residing. A family of dogs seemed perfectly normal in the huge kitchen where the older boys, their pale blond, almost white hair glistening in the artificial light, were pulling on heavy socks and boots, the daughter-in-law was apathetically loading the washing machine, the dryer was already whirling with the previous load of washing, and a small but very pregnant cat was begging for her breakfast. An electric stove, nearly new, stood along one wall beside a monster refrigerator, nearly new, and a large upright freezer, also nearly new. On a counter along another wall were placed every electrical kitchen appliance known to man, as well as a rack of expensive-looking knives and an array of canisters. An elaborate spice rack was well filled. Near the door, beside the laundry appliances, coats, boots, scarves and mittens awaited anyone who would venture out of doors.

But the obvious center of the kitchen was the old-fashioned wood stove, a huge one with warming oven above. When Erica had hung up her parka, she stretched her hands out toward its warmth and couldn't help but smile.

"Pretty nice, huh," Jackie shouted over the prevailing din of dogs, cats, radio, television blaring in another room, and people clamoring for attention. "It was my mom's. I told her, 'Mom,' I says, 'You've got to will me that stove. Don't let no one else have it.' I didn't have to wait for her to die after all, 'fore I got it. Mom, she had to go into the nursing home two - three years ago and we closed up her house. Jess built me this kitchen and we moved the old stove over here. I don't use it none for fancy baking, only for biscuits or roasts and such. I use the 'lectric range when I bake a cake. And I don't use it none in the summertime, but it sure beats the other one in the winter. We been living around it these last few days."

"I can imagine."

"Makes it nice for the pups, too. Eddie Lee, show Doc Merrill them pups. They sure have growed."

The boy shyly picked up a puppy and brought it to Erica for inspection. It did, indeed, appear healthy and fat. She had to admire each puppy in turn, and to pet Queenie who hovered anxiously beside her. Then with all the canines restored to the converted woodbox, Erica picked up the pregnant cat.

"She's thin," Erica remarked.

"Yeah, I know. I can't git any weight on her. I 'spect she'll git it back after she's had the kittens."

Erica turned the cat around and looked under her tail. "She has tapeworms," she told Jackie. "See those segments?"

"Oh! Guess I'd better give her some garlic."

"I don't think that would do much good. I've got some tapeworm medicine in my bag here. I'll give her a pill if you want."

"Sure. Why not?" Jackie was always easy to please. Erica extracted a bottle of tablets from her bag, shook one out into her hand, opened the cat's mouth and poked the pill gown her gullet. The cat scampered away.

"What are you feeding her?"

"Lots of scraps and fresh milk from Eugene's cow."

"What about commercial cat food?"

"Naw. None of that stuff. There's no need when we got all this stuff left over. How'd she get them worms. I heard they can git worms from drinking milk."

"No! Not at all. They get the kind of worms she had from eating rodents."

"What are rodents?" Eddie Lee inquired.

"Mice. Rats. Gophers."

"Oh, she catches lots of them."

"Well, then, you are going to have to worm her fairly often. You saw what those tapeworm segments looked like, didn't you?"

The boy nodded. "What's a 'segment'?"

"A piece. Tapeworms are a long string of those individual pieces. The head is fastened to the wall of the intestine and the pieces at the tail end break off and are passed out of the body. The pill I gave will make the head let go so the whole worm will come out."

"Oh!" Eddie Lee hung avidly on Erica's every word.

"Nice subject of conversation before breakfast," Jackie shouted. Her ample bosom shook with laughter. "Would you like to wash up before you eat?"

"Yes, please."

"Eddie, you show Doc Merrill where the bathroom is. And you wash your hands too. You been handling them pups."

All the while this was going on, Jackie was busily preparing breakfast. She said that Jess had eaten his and gone to work. They were still plowing the back roads and hoped to have them done that day. "Just in time for another storm," Jackie said, accompanying the words with another peal of laughter.

She opened the oven, from which a blast of heat washed across the kitchen, and popped a pan of biscuits into it, leaving another pan to be put in the oven later. She placed a huge cast iron skillet on the front of the stove where it was hottest and emptied a whole package of sliced bacon into it. When the bacon began to sizzle, she moved the skillet toward the back of the stove. As the meat fried, she would from time to time tilt up the skillet, press the grease out of the bacon with a spatula and pour it off into another pan. Into this second pan, once it was bubbling with bacon drippings, she broke a dozen eggs, and as they cooked, she basted them with the hot grease. She removed the bacon to a heated platter which she placed in the warming oven, built above the cooking surface, and slid the eggs, grease and all, onto another platter. Into the bacon skillet, she added a fistful of flour, letting it brown slightly over the hot stove. She poured milk from a pitcher into the pan and stirred the gravy industriously while it thickened. A pot of coffee stood on the back of the stove, keeping warm. When the first pan of biscuits was ready to come out of the oven, Jackie announced that breakfast was ready.

The daughter-in-law set five places at the table. "Aren't you going to eat with us?" Jackie asked.

"No, I'll get something later," the thin, anemic girl responded. By that time, Erica could sympathize with her. The smell and sight of grease was beginning to make her stomach queasy.

"This here's Crystal, Luke's wife." That was the only introduction Jackie seemed to think was necessary. The two women nodded to each other. Informality reigned. Luke, Erica knew, was the eldest Dibble son, now residing in the state penitentiary in Boise.

The two boys next in age, Zack, aged eighteen and Cody, fifteen, loaded their plates with three eggs apiece, eight or ten slices of bacon, three or four biscuits, which they crumbled onto their plates, and covered the whole works with copious quantities of gravy. Erica knew she had better take two eggs, or Jackie would be insulted, but she tried to transfer them to her plate without the accompanying bacon grease. She took three strips of bacon and two of the light, fluffy biscuits, which smelled very appetizing.

"Buttermilk biscuits," Jackie said. "*Real* buttermilk."

Real buttermilk had no special appeal for Erica since she knew that it was merely the residue of cream after all the fat had been turned into butter, and was thin and pale blue in color. But she had to admit that these biscuits smelled delicious, and when she had spread them with plenty of home-churned butter and had taken her first bite, she could have finished her breakfast on those alone.

The two older boys hunched over their plates, shoveling in the food with forks held tightly in their fists.

When, during the meal, the talk turned naturally to the murder, she saw the boys pause slightly, then lean even closer to their plates and put away their food at an even faster pace. She also noticed their mother's darting look in their direction. *Oh, oh! Something's up! Those boys were up to something that night, and Mother knows it,* Erica thought. She knew the boys' reputation and wondered about their relationship with their deceased neighbor.

The three older Dibble boys were all bullies, thieves and mischief-makers. Luke had graduated to the big time, and Clay Caldwell had told Erica that the next two were not far behind. He had called this household a crime factory.

Jess, the father, everyone thought surreptitiously stole from the county, but had never been caught at it. The big-screen TV in the living room turned up at the Dibble household shortly after a similar one had disappeared on its way to the county-run nursing home. Jess had a bill of sale for it from a dealer in Lincoln, but people doubted if any money had changed hands. They suspected, but never proved, that Jess had traded the one for the nursing home for one of a different make. It was thought that he had furnished almost his entire house in some such way. It was also thought that he used the county snowplow to open lanes and driveways for friends, collecting a fee, which he did not pass on to the county. There were other ways Jess could pick up a buck or two, all under the table, all unprovable.

Clay Caldwell thought he could probably pin something on Dibble if given a chance, but the man was, in other ways, an asset to the county; a hard worker, reliable, and one who maintained the equipment he used in good condition. He also possessed a powerful body and quick reflexes. Several young punks had thought they could whip him in a fight and had gone away like beaten dogs, with their tails between their legs, picking broken teeth out of their gums. As a thief, Jess was sly; as a fighter, he was dirty. His sons had inherited his mean streak and his desire to make a living off someone else's labor, but not his cunning and craft.

But there was one Dibble who didn't fit the mold. Tracy, the only girl, in between Luke and Zack in age, had been a quiet girl who receded into herself whenever she was approached, who had done well in school through sheer hard work, while all the older boys had dropped out. As soon as Tracy collected her diploma, she left Boulder, went to Lincoln and got a job. There she met a boy, Shaun Wilson, made a play for him and to her immense relief, he asked her to marry him. She had never come back to Boulder, where she had always been known as "the Dibble boys' sister." She hated it. The Wilsons had moved to Spokane where they became lost in the anonymity of several columns of Wilsons in the phone book.

Now the final member of the Dibble household toddled into view. Erica had never previously seen Crystal's little girl and when she did, she had difficulty hiding her surprise. The child had a head of spun silver hair and eyes so pale as to be almost colorless. Luke was blond like Jackie, but not the nearly white blond of his albino father and brothers. He was also blue-eyed, but did not have the pale washed-out eyes of the others. Crystal appeared to be blond, but Erica suspected the assistance of peroxide. Could two normal blondes have an albino child? Could albinism skip a generation? Was this, indeed, Luke's child? Erica had a vague memory flitting about in the back of her mind that rumor was that Luke had "gotten the girl in trouble" and had been forced to marry her. But no one cared about that any more. Lots of single women had babies. Was this case different because of the possibility that the baby's appearance would declare who the father was? Was that father Jess Dibble? What did Jackie know?

Whatever Jackie knew, it seemed to have no bearing on the way she treated the child. The baby tripped and fell, bumping her head. She sat there and wailed and Jackie paused in the act of taking the second pan of biscuits out of the oven to scoop up the child, kiss the spot that had been bumped and say, "Now it's all better. Gram-maw give the baby a biscuit." She held the child on her hip while she sliced open a hot biscuit, buttered it and spread it with honey. She set the child down and gave her the treat. The little girl grasped it in both hands, honey dripping between her fingers. "Now run along and eat it," Jackie cooed.

When Erica looked up again, she received another jolt. Eddie Lee was watching her and when her gaze fell on him, he gave her a shy smile. She saw that his eyes were brown, and that his once-blond hair was gradually turning brown. Was this the child of an albino father and a blond, blue-eyed mother?

Tit for tat, Erica thought. Had Jess responded to being cuckolded by getting a teen-age girl pregnant and forcing his son to marry her?

The night had passed and sunlight inched its way downward through the trees. Jackie busied herself with Eddie Lee's lunch. She ladled some vegetable soup from a large pot into a small pan and set it on the stove to heat. She took a baked ham from the giant fridge, cut a thick slice, placed it between two pieces of homemade bread, one slice buttered, one spread with mayonnaise. From the crisper she obtained a lettuce leaf and added it to the sandwich, putting the whole works into a baggy. She pulled a cherry pie from the fridge, cut a piece and wrapped it in plastic. Pouring the hot soup into a thermos, she packed everything into the lunch pail, along with a plastic fork and soup spoon.

Zack lounged near the door, waiting impatiently for Cody to finish eating. Glancing out the window, he announced, "There goes your school bus, Ed." A small van made its way on up the road. It would go to a farm a half mile on up the ridge, turn around and come back.

Cody glanced across the table at his small brother and laughed. "But if you go to school with that mustache, they'll send you home to shave."

Eddie Lee giggled as he ran his tongue along his upper lip to remove his mustache of milk. Cody cuffed him playfully and Eddie Lee grinned in delight.

"Cummon," Zack called. "Let's go feed them dogs." In the distance, Jess Dibble's cougar hounds were baying for their breakfast.

"Can I go with you sometime when I don't hafta go to school?"

"Them dogs would eat you alive," Cody told his younger brother, then growled fiercely, sending the boy into gales of laughter. He got up, collected his coat and followed Zack out into the cold. They disappeared down a trail into the woods.

Eddie Lee pulled on his boots and squirmed into his coat while his mother fetched cap and mittens. She clinked some coins into his pocket. "There's your milk money. Don't lose it."

"Ah, Mom! I like our milk better."

"I know, but I put hot soup in your thermos, so you'll have to buy milk."

Having made his point, Eddie Lee promptly forgot about it and hurried over to say good-bye to Queenie.

"Hurry up. Your bus will be here. Don't forget your books."

The small figure raced out of the house and down the driveway. He stopped on the near side of the road until the van's woman driver had stopped and signaled him to cross. He ran across the road and bounded into the bus.

"You know, he's the only one of my kids who's ever liked school. He can't wait to go," Jackie mused, watching her youngest dash off to get into the school bus.

Erica became aware of a jarring sense of dislocation, as if she was seeing a picture torn in two and crudely put back together. Here was a family which on the surface should delight the old conservative folk who decried the loss of "family values." In this family, the hard-working father was a good provider. The mother stayed home, feeding and caring for her brood, happily accepting into the flock a daughter-in-law and a grandchild. She cooked them large and tasty meals, clothed them with proper duds for the season, hugged them to her bosom, kissed their minor hurts, took care of their numerous pets and liberally scattered love indiscriminately about. Older brothers looked out for and played with their younger sibling. Yet probably at least half of them would one day land in jail.

Even with the boys gone from the room, the noise level remained intense. Glancing into the living room, Erica could see the back of Crystal's head. Lounging in an easy chair, the girl watched TV, its volume turned to the maximum, while in the kitchen, country and western music wailed from a radio. Jackie shouted to Crystal that her load of laundry was done. The baby gurgled happily in a corner of the room.

"Did you hear the shot Saturday night?" Erica asked over the din.

"What's that?" Jackie shouted.

"Never mind," Erica replied, her question answered. A war could start in their front yard, but this family would never notice.

On her way back to her vehicle, she could hear the deep baying of the hounds and more distant, the higher pitched barking of other dogs. She had wondered why the older boys had impressed on their little brother that it was not safe for him to go near the dogs. Hounds are not vicious; they are gentle dogs, trained to track, not attack. If anything, they might drown you with their copious slobber; but bite you? No! So why the warning? And were those other dogs she could hear on the Dibble property?

On her way out to the road, Erica paused beside a corral where two shaggy pack horses munched on hay, good alfalfa hay, dairy cattle hay. She remembered the large amount of milk, cream and butter in the Dibble kitchen and vowed to go up to Eugene's barn to see how the cow and calf were faring.

But first, she would visit Lena Lemm, who lived directly across the road from the murder site.

CHAPTER 10

From the Dibbles', Erica drove up the road to the next property. This rough, unimproved acreage was nonetheless surrounded by a stout, well-maintained three-strand barbed-wire fence. The ubiquitous cattle guard spanned the gap in the fence where an unimproved track led into the trees to the site of Lena Lemm's trailer. The track was not plowed, but another vehicle had been along it, probably the sheriff's Blazer. Directly across the road from Eugene Pettijohn's neat cabin, Lena's trailer could not have been more of a contrast. Her fences might be in good repair, but her home was not. Sections of siding were beginning to pull away at the corners, the roof revealed tar paper patches, and one board was missing from the step. Derelict farm equipment rusted in the yard. A battered old Dodge pickup truck sat forlornly in a lean-to. Only the tools, hung in an open shed, were well kept.

"Come on in," Lena boomed in her deep voice. "Watch that there step."

Standing five feet ten, big boned and running to fat since she no longer did a man's work fourteen hours a day, Lena seemed to fill all the space left in the trailer that wasn't piled with junk. She had run a small cattle ranch by herself for years after her husband had been killed in an accident. She had the muscles of a man and the rolling gait of a cowpuncher. She wore blue jeans, cowboy shirts and boots, and was reputed to be able to handle mules better than any man in the county. Ultimately her back gave out on her, and when she could no longer hoist a bale of hay, she had called it quits, sold the ranch and bought the acreage on Black Bear Ridge. She moved a stack of magazines off a chair and invited Erica to sit. "I've got coffee on. Want some?"

"No thanks. I'm all coffeed out. I hope I'm not disturbing you."

"No, no. I'm glad to have someone stop by. This time of year, I get cabin fever. Don't see no one for a week at a time. Only when I go to town to get groceries. That won't be a while yet, 'cause I can't get my pickup started in this weather."

"Can I bring you anything? Or better yet, I could drive you into town."

"I'd sure appreciate it if it ain't too much bother. Let me just finish this cup of coffee and put my boots on." She seemed to be dressed for the outside already, which wasn't surprising considering the chill drafts swirling along the floor.

Erica came right to the point. "You're right across from Eugene's place. Did you hear a shot Saturday night?"

"No, I didn't. That nice young deputy fella asked me that. Hell, the wind was roarin' up a storm and stuff was knocking around the yard. I couldn't hear myself think."

"How about before the storm started?"

"I was watchin' one of them gangster movies on TV. There was so much shootin' goin' on in it, I couldn't of told the difference."

"What about after the storm?" Erica mentally crossed her fingers. She held her breath, waiting for Lena's answer.

"I didn't hear none. But I'd gone to bed and I sleep real sound."

Erica slowly let her breath out. Would even a sound sleeper fail to hear a rifle shot? A person like Lena, who had spent years with her ears attuned to abnormal noises in the night, would recognize that the bark of a big hunting rifle reverberating across the landscape would be out of place. It was only a couple hundred yards to Eugene's cabin — well

103

maybe three hundred yards — and in the stillness and cold that followed the storm, when the authorities said the murder must have been done, sound could travel for miles. It wasn't proof, but Erica could easily convince herself that the shot had not been fired after the storm.

"I hear tell that you don't believe Herb Schultz shot him," Lena remarked, testing the temperature of the coffee in her mug with a noisy slurp.

"No, I don't. I wouldn't be surprised if he shot Eugene, but not in the way Lyle Kline thinks it was done. He's not smart enough, and he wasn't sober enough."

Lena scratched behind an ear, frowned, and commented, "Yeah, I think you're right. Only thing is, them two didn't get along.

"He's not the only one who didn't get along with Eugene."

"Yeah, you're right. None of the loggers got along with Eugene. Hell could freeze over before them loggers would be friendly with them envirmetist or whatever they call themselves."

How about the Dibble boys? Did Eugene ever have a run-in with them?"

Lena gave a hoot of laughter. "You bet he did! I 'member a time several years ago, when I first come here, a yearling Eugene was raisin' for beef up and disappeared. Someone cut the fence. Eugene accused them Dibbles; it'd have been Luke and his dad I reckon, but they couldn't pin nothin' on 'em. Then he's always complainin' about somethin' those other two boys have done. He complains about them there dogs barkin', too; not about the noise, but 'cause he figgers they ain't bein' cared for proper. Then they was always trying to get aholt of Eugene's cat, that there Simonize thing. I hate to think what they'd of done with it if they had. Throwed it in the dog's pen most likely. Say! Where is that cat now?"

"We have it down at the house."

"Oh, good. It was a nice pussy, even though I don't cotton to that kind of cat."

"Have you ever had trouble with the Dibble boys?'

"Yeah. Not much though. I ain't got nothin' that they want, and I kinda lay low and don't provoke them none, so they mostly leave me alone. That young'un comes over ever now and then, but he's a nice kid. He's different from them older boys."

"I know. I was thinking that, myself."

"He's always been real likable. I remember when he was little. He was a real bodacious baby, always grinnin' and gigglin'. I hope he don't grow up like the others."

Amen! Erica thought. "What did you think of Eugene?"

"Oh, he was okay. He was sort of prissy, but I got along with him. Say, now! If you want to know some one who didn't get along with Eugene, it would be Bud Brinkerhoff. Them two was like two tomcats fightin' over a she-cat in heat."

"What about? Logging?"

"Yeah. You know Eugene. He's always after folks to preserve the trees, and Bud, he's the kind of logger what just knocks down anything that's in his way. Last summer, some guy hired Bud to log forty acres he had out on the Boulder Crick road, but Eugene talked this guy into hiring that horse logger from Big Canyon instead. Bud might of killed him right then if there hadn't been other folks around when he heard about it. That Bud, he's a little guy, but he's got a temper." Lena thought a moment, then added, "Redhead!" as if that explained everything. "He's loggin' some land out the Bear Crick road right now."

"Do you know where?"

"Naw. I don't know where abouts it is, but it's owned by the Dinnisons. I heard Dick Thom say he was goin' to take his rig out there while things was still all froze up and pick up them logs. Wanted to get them before it thawed or he'd never of been able to get in."

Erica dropped Lena off at the supermarket and went to her clinic. Nothing was happening, but Kelly had made a couple of appointments for the afternoon. Erica returned and found Lena waiting for her. They loaded the groceries and drove back out to Lena's trailer.

I ought to check on Eugene's cow and calf, Erica thought as she reached the road after dropping Lena off. To her surprise, she saw Clay Caldwell's pickup parked beside the barn. Pulling up behind his, she got out and went through the gate. Clay appeared at the barn door, a shovelful of manure in his hands.

"Hi. Thought I'd see how the cow was doing and found that no one's cleaned the barn since Sunday," he explained.

Erica laughed. "I came for the same reason. I wanted to see if the calf is getting enough milk."

"Well, they both look pretty hungry," Clay said, turning toward the two bovines, both lowing as if they thought it time to eat.

"I wonder if they're being fed all right?"

"I don't know. They shouldn't be hungry this early in the day. But there are several fewer bales of hay than there were, three at least."

"I know where those are."

Clay raised quizzical eyebrows.

"Jess Dibble's two packhorses are eating good alfalfa hay. I doubt if he bought it. The cow is being milked all right. Probably too much. I hope they're leaving enough for the calf."

Clay sighed. "I guess I'll have to go down there and speak to them. I'm going to start counting the bales of hay and come every day to check."

"Want some help here?"

"Sure. If you'll rake stuff out of the corners, I'll do the shoveling."

They finished cleaning the barn then found the sawdust pile under a tarp. Tipping off the accumulated snow, they hauled several wheelbarrow loads into the barn and spread it around. Then letting the cow and calf back in, they threw hay to them and watched them attack it greedily.

"They sure are hungry," Clay commented.

"Yes. They need more food in this weather, too. Are they getting any grain, do you think?"

"The level has gone down since Sunday, so I suppose they are."

"Unless that's also being fed to the horses."

"Yeah. Well, I'll put a stop to that."

*   *   *

Jackie saw Erica's Jeep turn up the road and stop at Lena's. She watched anxiously for it to leave, and when it did, she saw to her satisfaction that Lena was in it as well. Jackie donned warm clothing and left the house, hurrying up the road to Carl Nelson's trailer. She wanted to know what the talk was in the bars. Were her boys in any danger? They had gone out early Saturday evening and had come home furtively in the middle of the night, seeming upset. They said they'd gotten stuck in the snow, but Jackie doubted it. She wanted to know what they had been up to.

Asking Carl had its drawbacks. He would want her to go to bed with him before he would tell her anything. She didn't like sex with Carl. He was too rough and was only interested in his own pleasure. Not like Ernie...

Her mind went back to that summer ten years ago when Ernie Thom had come to Boulder to spend the summer with his brother Dick while recovering from the effects of chemotherapy for cancer. The two bachelors cooked their own breakfast and ate supper out, but Ernie had very little appetite and was thin and pale. Jackie, with her earth mother instincts, had gone to the Thom home with attractive and delicious smelling casseroles to tempt his appetite. Ernie not only enjoyed the food, he liked Jackie's company as well.

One thing led to another and they soon found themselves in bed. He still had *that* much energy!

It was one of those summers when Jess was working at the far end of the county and only came home about twice a month. Jackie knew he'd found a willing woman in the camp. Usually when he came home, he was a hungry lover. But that summer, he'd dump his gear and head for one of the bars. When he got home late at night, he was too drunk or too tired for sex. She found Ernie's advances welcome.

She carefully counted the days when it would be safe. She couldn't very well go to the store and buy contraceptives, nor could Ernie, without the whole town knowing about it. Toward the end of the summer Ernie was due to go back to Seattle for a check-up and talked her into one last fling. She tried to tell herself that it really was safe, but later when she missed her period, cold fingers of fear crept over her. Jess had never laid a hand to her, but she wondered if he would when he found out she was pregnant by another man.

Sure enough, he'd hardly said hello after a co-worker had dropped him off before he was heading for the door again. But Jackie blocked it.

"No you don't! You've left me here all summer and I ain't had no sex at all," she lied. "You don't leave this here house till you've come to bed with me. Let's hurry up before the kids gets home." She had unbuckled his belt and was unzipping his jeans. He gave in quite readily, a big grin on his face.

So when the baby was born, there was no way of knowing it wasn't his own. Fortunately it was a fair-haired baby, not dark like Ernie.

Jackie insisted on naming this one. They had agreed that Jess would name the boys and Jackie the girls. But there had been only one girl, so Jess agreed. Jackie thought of naming the baby Ernie, but that might have been too obvious, so she decided on Eddie Lee. Jess didn't like the name. Too wimpy, he thought. He hated his own name,

Jesse. Jesse James Dibble. He wouldn't let anyone use the full name, nor would he answer to "Whitey." He'd skinned a few knuckles in his childhood enforcing his point. He named his sons real manly names; Luke, Zack, Cody. Fighting names! Eddie Lee just didn't fit.

But, as only Jackie knew, Eddie Lee was not Jess' boy. He was Ernie's boy. And Ernie had been a patient and gentle lover, much different than the other men Jackie had known.

The next summer, with Eddie Lee in his carrier, Jackie had stopped in at Dick Thom's. When was Ernie coming back, she wanted to know. Oh, didn't she know, Dick had asked. Ernie had died of his cancer soon after Christmas. For the only time in her life, Jackie had truly mourned.

Now she had a weapon to use if Jess ever suspected that the boy's increasingly dark coloring meant that he had a different father. She was sure the little granddaughter was not Luke's child. Luke hardly knew the girl when Jess had taken him out back and talked him into marrying her. When Luke had come in, he was pale and had rubbed Ben-Gay on his shoulder. He'd hobbled around like an old man for a few days. Jackie wondered what Jess had on Luke and what means he had used to enforce it.

At that, it wasn't as bad as the beating Luke himself had inflicted on Zack a few years before. It was after Luke's first real fling in big-time, adult crime. He'd come home bragging about it to his younger brothers, who had in turn bragged to their friends at school. Someone had reported it. After a nasty night in the city lock-up, Luke returned home in a rage and beat Zack to a pulp. Cody would have been next, but like Falstaff, had decided that discretion was the better part of valor and had run off and hid until evening when Jess was home to protect him.

Jackie knew the little girl was not of her flesh and blood, but the child of her husband and a sleazy girl, hardly twenty years old. But that didn't keep her from cuddling the baby as if she were her own grandchild. It wasn't the child's fault, poor little mite!

She was out of breath from the exertion of hiking uphill in the snow when Carl let her in, and flopped into a chair to recover. Carl got her a cup of strong black coffee. She tasted it and made a face. She started to ask him questions, but as she had expected, he said, "First things first!' and guided her toward the bedroom.

Afterward, as he was pulling on his pants, he asked, "Now what was it you wanted to know?"

She told him her concerns. Yes, he knew the boys had been out; he'd seen them leave. The younger one had been driving the black four-wheel-drive pickup truck with the windowless canopy on the back, even though he was too young to have a driver's license. Where were they going? Carl didn't know. Did he know what they were up to? He hesitated for a moment before telling her he didn't, making Jackie feel that he was holding something back. Was there talk in the bars? Carl became vague, his big bland face clouding over. He wouldn't answer directly, but Jackie knew.

Yes, she had reason to worry about her boys.

CHAPTER 11

The other female member of the Dibble family had worries of her own. Tracy Wilson sat down to a final cup of coffee before dressing, taking the baby to the neighbor who cared for him, and going off to work. She had seen Shaun off to his tile-laying job. The baby rolled onto his face in his crib and Tracy leapt to her feet and scurried across the room to turn him over. She had read that babies shouldn't sleep on their stomachs and she was desperately anxious to do everything right for her precious child. Besides, what would Shaun do to her, she wondered, if anything happened to his baby while he was off at work? He didn't like Tracy to work and leave the baby with the neighbor, but the reality of their lives required that Tracy work to supplement Shaun's income, since his jobs were sporadic and unpredictable.

Tracy worked for a cement company, her hours being from ten to two. Even the half-time income, at minimum wage, was useful. She paid the neighbor by doing housecleaning for her. The office was a tiny one, above the area where the cement trucks loaded. It was a bare office, with a desk for her and one for the boss, who was out around the property more than he was in the office, some filing cabinets, a computer and two chairs. Truck drivers came in, and an occasional customer managed to find the way up to her perch. Whenever the door to the uninsulated room opened, it let in a blast of cold air. Tracy wore slacks, sweaters and heavy socks to work. Her fingers were often blue with cold in spite of the small electric space heater the boss provided for her. He was a nice man and he did not allow any of the drivers to give her a bad time. She was thankful for the job.

Yet, her constant dream was to land a job in a "real" office where she could dress up, where the decor would be attractive, where it would be comfortably warm in winter and cool in summer, and where a succession of attractive young male co-workers and customers would pause beside her desk to pass the time of day. Then she could put Bronson into a real day care center.

She leaned over the crib and eyed the baby lovingly. She had never given her family her address in Spokane, but had only sent a birth announcement by mail, with no return address. Her mother was okay, but she didn't want the stigma of her father's and brothers' reputations following her. She refused to give out her maiden name. Even Shaun had never met her family. She had a soft spot for Eddie Lee, but once when she had suggested tentatively to Shaun that they have her younger brother live with them, he had replied with jealousy even of the small boy. She'd dropped the idea at once.

Shaun was a jealous type. He didn't like her working around all those men. She walked as on eggs, careful of everything she said to him. He was her security. She didn't really love him. He'd been her ticket out of the world she'd been born into. She couldn't afford to lose him.

But she felt she needed another string to her bow. Shaun always left the car for her to use, and when she went to the Shell service station near the cement plant for gas, she noticed a young man who worked there. He was friendly, and she'd found out when he was on shift so she could always go when he would be there. He had curly brown hair, brown eyes, and a dimple in his chin. He was really good-looking, she thought, and always smiling and joking. The name stitched on his jacket was "Gary." He didn't wear a wedding band. Tracy always slipped the wedding ring off her finger before she drove in.

She thought of Gary as her insurance policy in case anything happened between her and Shaun. Meanwhile, she made certain Shaun never went to the Shell station for gas.

As she sipped her coffee, she leafed through the newspaper from the previous day, which the landlady passed along to her tenants after she was through reading it. A small item on an inside page caught her eye. The dateline said Boulder, Idaho. What had happened in her old home town to make the Spokane paper? She read the article and began to tremble.

Eugene Pettijohn, the Dibbles' neighbor had been shot to death. The body had been discovered by a neighbor. The police had a suspect in custody. She felt the hair on the back of her neck stand up, her guts tighten and sweat break out on the palms of her hands. One of her brothers had finally done the unthinkable.

*   *   *

Only a few clients straggled into the clinic that afternoon. Erica began to be seriously worried about her practice. Could she make a go of it? She told herself that the present conflict would blow over and things would get back to normal. She also reasoned that many clients would put things off because of the weather, and when it improved, they would be back. Again, she sent Kelly home early.

After she had left Black Bear Ridge that morning, she had gone to the courthouse, to find out the location of the Dinnison land. The clerk in the assessor's office, on hearing her request, had replied with a ready description and set of instructions and had brought out a map. Then she had said, "You won't find Bud out there today, though. You won't find him at home, either. He's gone to Lincoln to get parts for his Cat. He'll be out there working again tomorrow."

Erica stared at her in disbelief. Was this lady a mind reader or what? The idea of interviewing Bud Brinkerhoff was only beginning to form in her own mind. She had thought of telling Clay what Lena had told her about Bud, but found herself rejecting that choice. Would the sheriff's office merely submerge this clue along with others that did not directly point to Herb Schultz? She realized that she was probably being unfair. Still, having decided that she was going to solve this case herself (just how she was going to do it was a subject she resolutely put out of her mind), she wanted to keep her clue to herself. Besides, she rationalized, the sheriff probably knew all about Bud's run-in with Eugene.

Perhaps she would go out there and interview Bud. It would depend, Erica told herself, on the weather and on whether her practice picked up again. Continuing cold would keep the road passable; a new snowfall would make driving very difficult.

One of the clients who came that afternoon had a toy poodle with a mouthful of rotten teeth. "He won't eat," the client told Erica. "I can't get a thing into him. And he stinks."

No wonder, Erica thought as she noted the puss oozing around the base of teeth that were held in place mainly by thick layers of tartar. She suggested that the client leave the tiny dog overnight for fluid and antibiotic therapy, and have the dental work done in the morning. *There goes my trip to see Bud Brinkerhoff,* Erica told herself.

The client frowned. "Dr. Somers told me he couldn't go under anesthetic because he's so old and his heart is bad. He's on some medicine for his heart."

This was no news to Erica. The small male Poodle was the archetypal animal to have heart disease, and the first thing Erica had done was to apply a stethoscope to his chest. The familiar squishy sounds of congestive heart failure, caused by the valves of the heart not closing properly, proclaimed that this dog was true to form.

"I know. But he can't survive without. I do dentistry on dogs with bad hearts all the time. With our modern anesthetics, they come through it all right. One can't say there is no risk, but in this case, the risk is worth taking because he won't live long with all that infection in his mouth."

The client reluctantly agreed, kissing the dog good-bye, which made Erica gag.

She spent the evening running down the stairs to the clinic every half hour to check on her depressed little patient.

On Wednesday morning, she gave the dog a bare minimum of pre-anesthetic tranquilizer, just enough to keep him from fighting the anesthesia mask. She let him breathe pure oxygen before she started the anesthetic. He went under with frightening speed, and Erica frantically shoved the tracheal tube down his throat and hooked him back to the oxygen supply. Gradually over the next few minutes, his heartbeat became more even and his gums became bright red. Soon his heart sounded better than it had before the anesthetic, the oxygen doing its work.

The teeth were finger loose, falling out as she touched them. Only a few needed to be pulled with forceps.

"Well, he's an old gummer now," Erica sighed, eyeing the toothless mouth. He was slow to wake up — poor kidneys and liver, no doubt — but eventually raised a shaky head, then gradually pulled himself to his feet.

"Trent says you always ought to do a whole bunch of lab work before you do dentistry," Kelly remarked.

"Ideally, yes. But that would delay getting the work done, since we have to send it to Lincoln, and anyway, I *know* he's going to have the other problems and take that into account. Besides, people won't pay for it. These people wouldn't have agreed if I'd tacked another seventy or eighty dollars onto their bill."

"Yeah," Kelly laughed. "That usually happened. So Trent went ahead and did the dentistry anyway."

By ten thirty, the little dog was romping around his cage, begging for attention — or food. "Give him a very small amount of mashed up canned food," Erica instructed Kelly.

The dog gulped it down and looked for more.

"Amazing," Kelly exclaimed.

The phone had rung twice while they were occupied with the dentistry. One caller had not left a message, but the other had. Erica quickly recognized Lena Lemm's deep, booming voice. "Say, if you're going out there to talk to Bud, I'd like to go along. I need to get outta the house."

At the time, Erica disregarded the call, but as her patient continued to scamper around his cage and eat everything put before him, Erica decided she could safely send him home. She called Lena and arranged to pick her up at noon. An hour to get to the Dinnison place and an hour back. Half an hour to talk to Bud. They could make the trip in daylight.

She found Lena waiting for her by the road. Lena carried in her hand a gun belt and holster, with a .22 revolver, built to look like a Colt .45, tucked into it.

"Thought I'd bring the gun along and do some target practice if that's okay with you," Lena said through the open door of the Cherokee. Seeing Erica's frown, Lena continued, "It ain't loaded." To reinforce this remark, she pulled the gun from its holster, broke it open and displayed the empty cylinders.

Erica nodded. "Okay."

Lena climbed in, settling herself in the bucket seat with a sigh. She set the holstered gun on the floor between her feet.

"Seat belt!"

"Oh. Okay. I never use them things myself." Lena searched for the end and buckled herself in.

As Erica made ready to pull back out onto the road, she paused for a large logging truck to pass. A big green Kenworth self-loading rig, its monster crane attached to the body behind the cab, it had the name "Dick Thom" and a phone number painted on the door.

The truck stuttered to a stop on the snow-covered road. Dick rolled down the driver side window and called out, "Hi, Erica. If you're going up to talk to Bud, the road's in good shape. I've been over it twice since it snowed. I don't think you'll even need chains."

"Thanks Dick. I've got them along anyway."

Could you even sneeze in this town without everyone knowing it?

The truck went on its way. As Erica headed up the road, she glanced at Lena. "Did you tell anyone I was interested in talking to Bud?"

"Yeah. Why?"

"Well, the whole town seemed to know it before I did myself."

"Yeah. I saw that woman what runs the day care place, you know, the daughter of that woman what works at the courthouse, and I told her."

"The one from the assessor's office?"

"Yeah. Her daughter. Can't remember her name."

That explained it then. Erica was not too pleased to have her actions chronicled all over town.

The road climbed over a low divide, then entered a long series of mountain meadows strung along a small creek. At the far end stood the buildings of another Boulder pioneer family. The Merrills and Lairds had homesteaded their two benches at the turn of the century. Twenty years later, old man Dunbar, as he was known locally, had bought up all the meadowland along Camas Creek and started the Camas Meadow Cattle Company. There had been Dunbars at the ranch ever since, and one of the girls had been Erica's bosom chum all through their school years.

The buildings, with their Christmas card picturesqueness, blended into the snowy backdrop. Erica relived fond memories as she drove past. These were the memories that made returning to her childhood home something she had always planned to do. But would it work?

"Why don't we stop in and say hello to the Dunbars on our way back?" Erica suggested.

"I'd rather not," Lena answered firmly. There was a set scowl on Lena's face and Erica caught herself just before asking why not. She didn't want to delve into Lena's problems. In a way, Lena was to the female population of Boulder what Herb Schultz was to the male. There were those who liked her and those who did not. There were a few like Erica who could see the good things about this horsy woman and accept the bad along with them. The bad included a propensity to gossip along with a disregard for repeating things accurately; also a tendency to go on the occasional drunken binge.

Lena, a non-stop talker, rumbled on, "My grandpa used to work for old man Dunbar. Slave driver, that man was. Worked the guys like horses. Grandpa said onct that he might as well of fed them hay and oats. Did you know him?"

"Know who? Your grandfather?"

"No. Dunbar."

"I met him once when I was a small child. He was pretty old and feeble by then."

"He wasn't when he was younger. Great big bear of a man. Could do the work of two ordinary guys. So could my grandpa. He had to show off and try to outwork the old man. He looked like Charles Bronson, you know that actor what made the movie in these parts several years ago. Can't remember the name of it. Something about heartbreak."

"*Breakheart Pass.*"

"Yeah, that's it. Did you know that the Dibble girl named her kid after him? Bronson, she calls him."

"Do you mean Tracy Dibble?"

"Yeah. Got married to some guy down in Lincoln and moved to Spokane. Won't come home. Jackie told me. Did you know he had a mistress somewhere up here in the woods?"

"Who did?" Erica asked, running back over the names of the men Lena had been talking about. Tracy's husband? Charles Bronson? Lena's grandpa? Old man Dunbar?

"Dunbar. That guy I was talking about."

Erica shut off the flow of words that came into her ears from the part of her brain that would have to analyze them. Lena had the effect of producing a sort of aural paralysis after a period of time. Erica never did find out who it was that had looked like Charles Bronson.

Plunging into the forest again, the road climbed ever upward. After the sun reflecting brilliantly off the snow in the open meadow, the gloom of the thick forest seemed exaggerated. The green-black trees, made into grotesque shapes under their mantle of snow, made the landscape seem forbidding. There was no color. All was black or white. Dazzling, blinding white. Deep, impenetrable black shadow. The contrast made Erica's eyes ache.

Eventually, she turned off onto a side road, still traveled well enough to make the driving easy. After about two miles, she began to look for the logging road off to the left. It was not difficult to find. Dick's big rig had churned up the snow, leaving a massive scar in the fleecy blanket that lay thick on the ground. Shifting down and using the four-wheel drive, Erica made her way cautiously up the track. Dick had been right. His huge rig had flattened the snow, leaving firm tracks in which the Cherokee had no difficulty. Where Dick had loaded his logs, Erica stopped, heading her vehicle down the road toward home. She and Lena climbed out. They could hear Bud's Cat up in the timber.

Lena strapped on the gun belt, loaded with ammo. Pulling shells from the belt, she shoved them into the cylinder of the revolver. Six of them; not letting the hammer rest on an empty one. Erica felt a sudden queasy rush of doubt. What had she agreed to? Here she was, miles and miles out in the wilderness in the middle of winter, with a person who might well be a suspect in a murder case and who knew she was investigating it. That suspect now stood beside her, calmly loading a gun.

If she shoots me now, Erica thought, my body won't be found until late in the spring.

CHAPTER 12

Erica and Lena passed Bud's parked truck, skirted the pile of logs that he had already skidded down to the road and followed the tracks of the Cat up a hill into the timber. After about a quarter of a mile, they came to a small clearing where it appeared that Bud kept the tractor when he wasn't using it. The snow here was packed down and covered with tracks. Empty oil cans, bright yellow in color, had been discarded by throwing them into the brush at the edge of the clearing. Small trees had been knocked over and bulldozed out of the way. The 'dozer blade sat in the snow at the edge of the clearing. A brown paper bag and a couple of sandwich wrappers drifted across the clearing before a light breeze. A plastic grocery bag, caught in a tree branch, rustled as the wind caught it. Assorted other bits of junk littered the scene.

Erica wondered what else lay under the snow, since obviously Bud had been logging here for some time before the storm. *I can understand why he and Eugene Pettijohn didn't get along,* she thought.

The sound of the Cat came closer, off to the left, and soon the big yellow machine appeared out of the trees, several logs in tow. Bud was looking back at the logs as he rounded a corner, being careful not to snag his load. He drove straight ahead, waiting for the logs to clear the surrounding trees before turning down the hill. He did not turn around so he could see the two women until he had driven well into the clearing. When he did, he abruptly stopped the Cat, brought the throttle to idle and sat unmoving in the seat, waiting for Erica to make the next move. He was a man of slightly under average height, beginning to put on a pot belly, with a round face, crew-cut red hair, blue eyes, freckles and a turned-up nose. Under his winter jacket he wore a faded navy blue sweatshirt with a hood. The drawstring of the hood was tied firmly under his chin. His face, glowing red with the cold, held a wary expression.

Erica strode purposefully across the clearing toward the Cat, vaguely aware that Lena had stayed behind. She stopped beside the machine and looked up into Bud's unwelcoming face.

"What do you want?" Bud growled. Erica remembered Lena's description of his personality. Her stomach gave a small spasm of protest. She hadn't really thought out what she would ask him. Her idea of taking a firm stance and asking deliberately provocative questions now seemed a bit foolhardy. She swallowed, and plunged in.

"I understand you and Eugene Pettijohn had an argument," she stated with as much conviction as she could muster.

But the logger didn't seem to have heard her. He stared over her shoulder. His gaze came back to Erica's face with a start.

"What?" he asked.

Erica repeated the question. Bud's attention seemed to have wandered again and he answered distractedly, "Yeah. But it didn't mean nothin'."

"I understood that it was quite a heated argument."

Bud brought his attention back to Erica's face and answered in a tone that indicated a desire to please, "Well, that was all bluff. It didn't mean nothin'. Eugene was an all-right guy. I was just edgy that day."

"That's not what I heard."

Bud's attention was elsewhere again. He seemed intent on a spot somewhere over Erica's right shoulder. He brought his focus back with a start.

"Don't pay no attention to what folks say. I didn't mean no harm." He was almost pleading. As Erica debated what to ask next, Bud edged out of his seat toward the far side of the Cat, tense as a fully stretched door-spring.

BANG! BANG! BANG!

Erica whirled around, but not before she had seen Bud leap off the far side of the Cat and disappear behind it.

There was Lena, holding the smoking revolver in her right hand, calmly walking over to the edge of the clearing to inspect three yellow oil cans which were not now in the same place they had been before. She tossed one into the air with her left hand, raised the gun and fired. The can skittered off in a new direction. Before it hit the ground, Lena fired two more shots, finding the mark both times.

"Hot damn! I can still do it!" she shouted. She broke open the gun, emptied the spent shells onto the ground to add to the general litter, and pushed six more into the holes in the cylinder.

"Hold on a minute, will you, Lena? I want to finish talking to Bud," Erica called out, laughing in relief. She'd been pretty startled herself by the burst of gunfire, and realized how tense she'd been.

"Okey dokey. Whatever you say."

Erica turned back toward the Cat.

"You can come out. She's only doing some target practice," she called out. Bud tentatively raised his head above the level of the machine's giant cleated track, a look of uncertainty on his face.

"Look here," he said. "I know you think I might of killed old Eugene, but I didn't. I swear it. I was home in bed that night. My wife can tell you."

"Nobody besides your wife?"

Bud shook his head, but the motion became tentative. He frowned as he concentrated his thoughts on the problem. "I think maybe one of the kids called."

"One of your kids called from Lincoln?" She knew that Bud was divorced and had teenage children who lived with his first wife.

"Yeah. But I can't 'member if it was that night. Prob'ly not. They'd have been out at a game or a dance or somethin'."

"Is there anyone else who could say you were home?"

"Don't know." Bud thought a moment, then gave Erica a calculating look. "Say! What right do you have…" His voice trailed away as he focused his gaze on Lena, standing there with her hands on her hips, the right one only inches from the holstered revolver. *He still thinks I brought Lena as an enforcer,* Erica thought.

"I'm only trying to get at the truth." Erica's tone was conciliatory. Furthermore, she thought she probably had it. Bud's answers didn't impress her as lies.

"Okay. Sorry to bother you," she said. "We'll stand over there out of the way so you can go past. We don't want to bother you."

They waited until the logs had disappeared down the hill, then Lena sent another oil can skittering across the snow until she had emptied the gun again. This time, when she dumped the shells, she did not reload.

*   *   *

After she dropped Lena off, Erica drove into the town to get gas at the Chevron service station. For once, its proprietor did not come out to greet her with a stream of jokes and witticisms. A teenage assistant filled the Cherokee's tank silently, with averted gaze, and had to be reminded to check the oil and wash the mud-splattered windshield. Erica herself had to get out and wash the back window. She handed the youth her credit card and waited interminably for him to bring it back, along with the slip for her to sign.

While she waited, another car pulled in on the other side of the pumps, and Erica recognized one of her favorite high school teachers, a local man, one of the McMurtrys. He called out a cheery greeting and they talked through the open windows of their vehicles.

"Come and have a cup of coffee with me at the café," the teacher called out.

"Okay," Erica readily agreed. After the long trip into the frozen wilderness, she could stand a hot cup of coffee.

They slid into a booth as far from the door as possible to avoid the cold rush of air when anyone entered. The waitress wore a sweater, but the cook poked her head out over the serving counter and called cheerily, "Hi, Mr. McMurtry. You outta be in this kitchen here. Only warm place in town." Everyone laughed.

"I come in here every afternoon for a cup of coffee. I usually sit at the counter and tease the cook. Its about the only social contact I have these days since the kids are away in Arizona."

Erica knew that "the kids" were Mr. McMurtry's middle aged son and daughter-in-law who lived in the big old McMurtry house, and that the retired teacher occupied the basement suite.

"Come over some afternoon for tea, Erica. Or should I call you 'Dr. Merrill' now?"

"*You* shouldn't. Some other people should."

"It's hard to get started in a town where you grew up, isn't it?"

"Yes, it is. I'm not sure I can do it."

"Of course you can. I've never seen you fail at anything yet." The old man smiled across the table and Erica was both touched and embarrassed.

"That sounds good," she said, "coming from my second favorite teacher."

"Only second!" he responded in mock horror. "Who is your favorite?"

"Your wife."

"Of course. Did you know you were her favorite student?"

"No!" Erica was genuinely surprised.

"You were. It was because of you that Emma asked to be transferred from teaching second grade to third. She wanted to have you in her room another year."

"I didn't know that. But I was certainly delighted when I found out that she would be my teacher again. My first grade teacher was sort of stifling. But Mrs. McMurtry let me do all sorts of extra things as long as I also got my regular schoolwork done. She was the first and last teacher in grade school or junior high who encouraged me like that. Then in high school, I had you for English and Mr. Kinch for science. Both of you let me spread my wings."

"And watched with joy while you did so."

A lump developed in Erica's throat and she found herself at a loss for words, a rare experience for her.

A man in logger garb entered the cafe, found a stool at the counter and ordered biscuits and gravy.

"That reminds me," Erica remarked, "I had breakfast at the Dibble's yesterday, and you wouldn't believe the food they eat."

"I probably would believe it, but what was it like?"

"Grease, salt, gravy on everything, far too much of everything, but the most delicious biscuits I've ever tasted, if you didn't smother them in gravy."

"I'm not surprised. That reminds me of another of Emma's projects. One less successful than her work with you."

"What was that?"

"The Dibble kids. Emma always took a personal interest in the children in her class. She looked for evidence that they were not well cared for; things like dirty clothes, no warm coats in winter, inadequate lunches, bruises. The Dibble boys acted like abused children, but they came to school in good clothing, warm coats and boots, always clean. They brought the best lunches of any children in the class.

"Generally speaking, you could, in those days, see a difference between the farm kids and the loggers' children. The farm kids had a better, more varied diet. Loggers tended to be meat and potato types. No vegetables. And meat only when the father bagged his deer or elk. They didn't eat a very good diet. Emma noticed that the farmers tended to be bigger and healthier and their children grew faster. She put it down to diet. The farm families had lots of fruit and vegetables in their diets, and fresh meat year-round. They had a more balanced diet and more of it. The loggers families, except those in which the wife raised chickens and grew a garden, were likely to subsist on beans and macaroni, especially in the winter when the father was laid off and there was no money to buy meat."

"That's an interesting thought. But those loggers make far better wages than most farmers have in income."

"Yes, but they didn't save. Easy come, easy go. When they were hauling in the big paychecks, they spent lavishly. But when logging stopped in the fall, they had nothing but unemployment checks, most of which went for booze and cigarettes. Mind you, I'm generalizing. Not all of them were like that."

"They still are like that. I have clients who come in now saying that they can't pay their bills because the payment has to be made on the four-wheel-drive pickup they bought last summer when they were working."

"Emma, God rest her soul, had a suggestion for that. She even made it to the local car dealer, but he wasn't interested."

"What was that?"

"She suggested that they schedule payments over an eight month period and make each payment fifty percent higher. They would get the same amount of money, without having to try to extract it from people when they were out of work."

"Someone should have taught these people how to budget."

McMurtry groaned. "You're right, but do you realize how hard that is?"

"To get back to the Dibbles. What were they like in school?"

"Little terrors. The boys were bullies and had absolutely no interest in learning. I don't think they were mentally retarded, but they had no encouragement at home. They were pretty smart when it came to avoiding work. Now Tracy, the girl, was different. She was unimaginative, but applied herself diligently and got decent grades. She will probably never advance much above simple jobs, but as long as employers want reliable workers, she will be able to find a job. Emma felt sorry for her. She didn't seem to enjoy life very much. And she hated to be known as Luke's sister. Poor girl."

"The youngest boy isn't like the rest, though. He enjoys school."

"I've heard that. It's too bad Emma isn't here to see it. She would have been relieved to know that one of the Dibbles had a chance to turn out all right." He paused for a moment, then went on, "He probably isn't actually a Dibble, though."

"Oh! You've noticed that, too?"

"It's fairly common gossip. Jackie Dibble is known to sleep around. Jess too, for that matter. The boy is probably not his. Emma would have been trying to get him out of that household into a more favorable environment."

As they left the café, McMurtry reminded Erica again of her promise to come to tea and they made a date for Friday. As they parted, it occurred to Erica that Alex McMurtry must have gone through the same process of trying to gain acceptance in his home town as she was now doing. He had certainly succeeded.

There was a difference, however. He was a man.

CHAPTER 13

Erica arrived back at her clinic at about four o'clock. As she entered, she could hear Kelly on the phone saying, "Here she comes now. Hold on a minute." To Erica, she called out, "It's Dr. Somers."

Erica went to her office, shedding her heavy parka as she walked. She picked up the phone and said "Hello" in a neutral, inexpressive voice.

"Hello, Erica. I called to find out if one of your former patients was vaccinated." He gave the name and Erica realized that this was the dog she was to have neutered the day before.

"Couldn't Kelly tell you?"

"Yes, she did, as a matter of fact. She said she'd send copies of your records on a couple other clients who are coming to me now, too."

"So what else do you want?"

"You know, Erica, you're not going to make a go of it there. You ought to go in with me. I'd do the large animal and we'd share the small. You could run the office. We could buy George out . . ."

"Forget it!"

"Why not?"

"You know damn well why not!"

"Erica, I don't like to hear a woman swear."

"Then hang up the phone. As a matter of fact, *I* don't like to hear a man swear. I also don't like pompous men who think a woman's place is doing office work. So don't worry about my practice. I can handle it."

"You don't seem to be doing a very good job, if I may say so. I've had several of your clients come to me this week."

"You can have them! Lotsa luck!"

"I'm just trying to help you."

"Oh yeah? Well then why don't you send my clients back to me?"

"They prefer to come to me. It's their choice."

"So it's their choice. Look, I've got work to do."

"One more thing, Erica. It's the reason I asked to speak to you."

"What?" Erica asked, failing to keep the belligerence out of her voice.

With all the assurance of the dominant male who expects all females to drop at his feet, Trent asked, "I called to invite you to the barbershop quartet concert tonight. I already have the tickets."

"Then you'd better find someone else to go with."

"I would like you to go with me."

"I'm not interested in barbershop quartets."

"Is that definite?"

"That's definite. I'm not going."

"Well, good-bye then. But think about my other offer."

"I don't have to think about it. Good-bye."

She slammed down the phone.

*   *   *

Kelly had two appointments booked, keeping Erica busy until nearly five. She called the owner of the little toothless Poodle and was told he had slept most of the afternoon, but was now begging for food.

"He hasn't eaten like this for a long time. I'm so glad you talked me into having his teeth pulled. But will he always go around with his tongue hanging out the side of his mouth?"

"Probably so."

"Oh, well! As long as he's happy. When should I start his heart medicine again?"

"Continue right on with it."

"All right, I will. Thank you, Dr. Merrill."

Erica was feeling less depressed than she had after Trent Somers' call. She closed the clinic and went upstairs. She could hear voices in the kitchen and on investigating found her brother, Wade, and his wife, Heather, seated at the kitchen table talking to Gram.

"Hi, Erey," Wade called out happily. "Here, have a chair." He got up and offered Erica his chair.

"Hi." Heather added her greeting. They were a cheerful couple and always raised Erica's spirits.

Wade leaned his broad-shouldered frame against the kitchen counter, looking taller than his five feet ten in his high-heeled western boots. He wore faded Wranglers with a hand-carved western belt and large oval trophy buckle, now dented and scratched, from some past rodeo. Over his wool shirt, he wore a sheepskin-lined denim jacket. A broad-brimmed western hat rested on the counter. He had inherited his father's heavy frame, though not his height; also his father's sandy hair, beginning to recede. Erica took after their mother in both stature and coloring. Both had the Merrill triangular face and had acquired a similarity of facial and vocal expression resulting from close association throughout their childhood. Heather often said, in a friendly, joking way, that the only woman she needed to be jealous of, in relation to her husband, was his sister.

"We came by to see if you and Gram would like to go to the concert tonight," Wade explained.

"The barbershop quartets?"

"That's right. What else is there?"

"Nothing much in this town. I just told Trent Somers I wasn't interested in going."

Heather smiled. "Wasn't interested in going, or wasn't interested in going with him?"

"Either one."

"Don't pay any attention to that. He's a drip. Go with us."

"Are you going, Gram?"

"Yes, I think I will. Now, I'm going upstairs to change while this roast finishes."

"Okay. Count me in. You can all surround me and keep me safe. Trent rather arrogantly suggested that I'm a failure, that I should give up my practice and run the office for him while he does the real work, that my clients are all going over to him. Then he has the audacity to ask me for a date."

"He needs a box on the ear," Heather opined.

Wade watched his grandmother leave the room, turned back to Erica and lowered his voice.

"I didn't want to say this in front of Gram, but we came to tell you we don't agree with what Dad wants you to do. Or not do. Erey, I think it's great that you're willing to stick up for someone that other people don't like. It's in our blood, anyway. Remember all the stories about our great-granddad defending the Indians? Not very popular in those days, but he was respected in the community just the same. Dad seems to have forgotten. He's so wrapped up in his politics."

"Thanks." It was all Erica could manage to say, what with the lump in her throat.

Heather picked up the thread of the conversation. "Your Dad is a wonderful person, but he does tend to think women can't take care of themselves. He still wants to saddle horses for me. Wade taught me how on my first trip here to visit him, and I'm an old ranch hand now, but he still thinks I'm something fragile that has to be handled with care."

Erica laughed. "He gave up trying with me years ago! But he still doesn't think I'm capable of making a decision. Gramp was the one who had faith in me."

Wade smiled. "I remember when I told Dad that I really didn't want to be a vet. I did it with Gramp there, because I thought he'd stick up for me. He did, but he really dropped a bombshell when he told Dad that there would still be a vet in the family." Wade turned toward Erica. "I guess Gramp was the first person you mentioned your interest to."

"That's right. I knew *he'd* understand."

"Dad was flabbergasted! He forgot all about me. I think eventually he realized that having another generation of rancher with an education was to the advantage of the ranch. He's always been ready to accept new ideas, and he's let me have my way on lots of things."

"Of course he does. You're a man. He wouldn't take it from me."

"I wouldn't say that. He's not that much of a male chauvinist. He's just gotten into this political thing, tapping into the old boy network and all that. Heather, if I ever start acting like that, stop me, will you?"

"I'll give you a quick kick in the shins."

"Anyway," Wade went on, "stick to your guns. You have our support, for what it's worth."

*   *   *

After the concert, which was held in the high school auditorium, the crowd filed into the gym for refreshments, naturally drifting into little groups. The Merrills had absorbed Bill and Patsy Clarke into theirs before Gram excused herself as she spotted friends on the other side of the hall.

"A night off from parenting!" Patsy Clarke exclaimed happily.

"Same here," Heather agreed. "Are Bill's folks minding the monsters?"

"Yes, they are. One advantage of living with your in-laws."

"Isn't it!"

The husbands spotted their old football coach, Stew Kinch, and abandoned the women, who themselves started searching for the refreshment table. They found it across the gym floor and began edging their way though the crowd. Everyone in Boulder, or so it seemed, was there.

Half way across the room, Erica found herself face to face with Jackie Dibble.

"Hi there! Hey, Eddie Lee! Here's Doc Merrill."

The small boy squeezed through the surrounding crowd and greeted Erica.

"He's decided he wants to be a vet. He wondered if you had any work he could do."

Erica had a sudden vision of her old teacher, Mrs. McMurtry, looking for some way to get this child out of his unhealthy home.

"Well, let's see. I could put you on as official dog walker and cat petter if you want to come over sometime. I can only pay you in Gram's homemade cookies."

The grin on the boy's face was acceptance enough.

"He could come after school and Jess can pick him up when he gets off work at four-thirty," Jackie suggested.

"That's fine." Erica looked enquiringly at Eddie Lee. "Tomorrow?"

"Oh, great!" the boy answered.

Erica and Patsy continued toward the refreshment table while Heather went to take orders from the men. They surveyed what was on offer, expecting to find the usual favorites—beef sandwiches, sausage rolls, brownies—and not espying them. Holding sway at an unappetizing assortment of comestibles was Marigold Considine, wife of a new young doctor recently ensconced in the town as a partner for old Dr. White.

"We have granola bars, peanut-yogurt cookies, whole-grain bread with just a touch of natural honey ..."

"Do you have any with unnatural honey?" Erica asked.

"What's that?" Mrs. Considine asked, having swallowed the bait.

There were sandwiches consisting mainly of alfalfa sprouts, ones with sliced chestnuts and yogurt, but not a speck of meat in sight.

"Is this all you have," Patsy asked.

"Yes. The Doctor says people eat too much fat and salt," Mrs. Considine expostulated. "The Doctor says that's why they have so much heart disease."

"I'm not an herbivore," Erica stated.

"The term is 'vegetarian'," Mrs. Considine corrected her.

"No the term is 'herbivore.' Being a vegetarian is a life-style choice. Being an herbivore is a matter of genetics. You know, the human race is the only species of animal that deliberately eats a diet that's not suitable for it. Others do when there's nothing else to eat, but we do it deliberately."

"What is an herbivore?"

"A cow."

"Oh." Mrs. Considine sucked in her breath and began again on her lecture. "The Doctor says . . ."

"What doctor do you work for?" asked Erica, maliciously.

"I don't work for any doctor."

"You keep saying 'The Doctor.' I assumed you worked for one."

"Dr. Considine is my *husband!*"

Patsy Clarke entered the fray. "*I* know what my husband's name is."

They drifted off, having bypassed the foods on offer. Heather had returned, but rather than joining them, she proceeded to the food table, executing a slinky walk with her tall frame.

"Good evening," she intoned. "The Rancher asked me to get him some of Mrs. Vanderpool's double chocolate brownies. I don't see them here."

"We don't have anything like that."

"Oh, dear. The Rancher will be disappointed."

Mrs. Considine turned her back on Heather and viewed the latest customer. Eddie Lee Dibble chinned himself on the side of the table and glanced about. He pointed. "What's that green stuff?"

"That's zucchini bread."

Eddie Lee wrinkled his nose. "YUCK!" He scurried away.

"I wonder if she has any saucers of cream. I could lap one up about now," Erica purred.

They bent over in gales of laughter.

"You know," Heather remarked, "if she were a nice person, someone would take her aside and in a friendly way explain to her that you don't try to sell a vegetarian diet to a bunch of cattle ranchers."

The men were still ensconced with their old coach and Erica noticed that Clay Caldwell had joined them. He was in civvies; tan cords, carefully creased, a brown plaid shirt open at the neck with a new white T-shirt showing, and a V-necked brown sweater. The brown clothing went well with his dun colored hair that lay in tight waves on his scalp. She could see him in profile and was struck by the fact that he had matured into a really handsome man.

She watched the group break up and the men look about for their women.

"I thought you weren't going to come." The statement was an accusation. Erica turned to face a scowling Trent Somers.

"Wade and Heather persuaded me to come with them."

"Yeah?" Trent glanced toward the approaching men. "And Caldwell too, I suppose."

"Actually not."

"Erica, I don't like your attitude."

"Well, I don't much like yours, either. By the way, I did dentistry on one of your cases." She gave the name. Trent seemed startled. "He's doing fine. The owners say he's like a new puppy."

"My God! You shouldn't put a dog like that under anesthesia."

"Maybe *you* shouldn't. But I'm well equipped and experienced in geriatric work." She turned away, walking toward the approaching men.

They all had long frowns on their faces.

"What's the matter with you guys?"

Wade replied, "Coach just told us that Charlie Oliver has dropped out of school."

"I thought he'd at least finish the basketball season."

"That's just it. He's gotten on with the Forks team."

"The Indian team? Isn't he rather young?"

"Yeah. But he's a natural, like Louie," said the other half of the Louis and Clarke combination. "I guess they wanted some more scoring punch. Charlie can hit baskets standing on his head. He would have broken all Louie's records if he'd stayed in school."

"There's a tournament at Forks this weekend," Wade explained.

Erica had a far-away look on her face. "You know, it might be fun to go watch it."

Clay stirred and entered the conversation for the first time. "Erica, just leave Charlie to me."

"Can't I go watch a basketball game?" she challenged. He shrugged and looked unhappy. *Why do we need to snap at each other?* Erica wondered. *I'd really like to get along with this guy.*

"Let's go," Heather exclaimed. "Wade keeps telling me what an exciting brand of basketball those Indians play. I'd like to see it."

Grinning, her husband agreed, and they made arrangements to pick up Erica. The Clarkes begged off, citing another commitment.

"I'm on duty," Clay remarked glumly.

As the center of gravity of the crowd began to shift toward the door, Erica saw Dr. Considine ambling their way, giving the food table a wide berth. Patsy noticed as well. "You know, I've seen him at Barney's Drive-in picking up a burger and fries several times."

Dr. Considine joined their group, a vaguely thoughtful look on his thin face. "If anyone had told me that I would be living in a place where a barbershop quartet concert was considered the height of culture, I'd have told them they were out of their mind."

"Wait until summer when we have our Art Fair and see what we think is the ultimate in fine art." Erica smirked.

"What?"

"Chain saw sculpture!"

CHAPTER 14

A client was waiting for Erica at eight the next morning. She recognized another rancher, a friend of Wade's. He had with him an Australian Shepherd dog, its thick blue merle coat glistening in the early morning sun.

"This here's Belle. She's passing a lot of blood when she pees," the rancher explained.

"How long has she been doing that?"

"Dunno. I didn't really notice till it snowed and you can see the blood in the snow. But she's been squatting to pee every few minutes for a while before that."

"Get her up here on the table and lets have a look at her."

Erica ran her hand down the abdomen and squeezed the area in front of the pelvis. She could feel something firm, something gritting, as she palpated. She parted the thick hair below the stub of a tail to see if the bitch was in season. She wasn't, so that wasn't where the blood was coming from.

"I think she has bladder stones. Let's get an X-ray."

"What'll you have to do if she does have stones?"

"Surgery. Remove the stones. Then put her on a special diet."

"Oh! That sounds expensive."

"Not too. Its not difficult surgery and she's a healthy dog otherwise. How old is she?"

"Five."

"Still relatively young. Here's what we should do. First get the X-ray to confirm that's what the problem is. I'm pretty sure, though. Then we should do some blood work and a urinalysis to see if there are any complications we need to be aware of. When I have the stones out, I should send one to the lab for analysis."

"Is that necessary?"

"Yes. There are different kinds of stones. We need to find out what kind she has so we can put her on the proper diet. Bladder stones are caused, at least partly, by diet. If she has phosphate stones, she needs to be on a diet that keeps her urine acid. But if she has oxalate stones, they form in acid urine, so she needs a different diet."

The rancher pushed back his hat and scratched his head. "Sounds complicated. But I guess you know what you're doing. Belle here, she's a real good dog. She works cattle as good as any dog I've ever had, and she throws good pups, too. All her pups have turned out good. I don't want to lose her, so you go ahead and do what you need to do."

"That's fine. Do you want to leave her, or bring her back tomorrow?"

"Can't you do it today?"

"Has she eaten this morning?"

"Yeah. She eats like a horse."

"I can't give her an anesthetic when she has food in her stomach. She might vomit and inhale some of it. Besides, I need to do the lab work before I do surgery."

"Well, I don't want to make an extra trip into town, so you keep her. She'll be okay, wont she? Them pups of hers bring a hundred dollars each."

"She should come through the surgery just fine."

"It won't keep her from having pups will it? You won't spay her?"

"No, no. I'd never spay a dog without the owner's permission. And the bladder surgery won't keep her from having puppies."

"Okay. Well, you do what you have to do."

When the rancher had left, Erica lay Belle on her side on the x-ray table and took a lateral view of the abdomen.

When developed, it clearly showed the bladder full of small stones. She assembled the lab materials. "I guess I'll have to take blood now, even if she isn't fasted, in order to catch the courier from the lab." A driver from a lab in Lincoln made a stop in Boulder at about eleven in the morning.

Erica shaved the hair off the front of Belle's foreleg, and as Kelly held her thumb across the vein, took a sample of blood. They then took the dog outdoors on a leash, Kelly following along behind with a pan. Sure enough, Belle squatted to urinate and Kelly shoved the pan under her to catch the urine. It was bright red with blood.

Belle, an outdoor cattle dog seemed delighted to be out of the heated house and flopped down in the snow, panting; her breath raising clouds of steam. Erica had one outdoor run for dogs. She hadn't used it since the beginning of the cold spell. She had Kelly put a heavy blanket in the run, but Belle sniffed it and spread herself full length on the bare concrete.

"Give her a bowl of hot water, and check every half hour to see if it's frozen."

Belle wagged her stub of a tail. She seemed perfectly happy. She watched the two women from one eye that was blue and one half blue, half brown.

"She has a nice temperament for an Australian Shepherd," Kelly remarked. "Some of them are pretty hard to get along with."

"I think the real working dogs are probably better than ones kept as pets. They're doing what they were bred to do. I suppose dogs need a sense of self-worth just like people do."

"Do you think so? I never thought of that."

They packaged the specimens for the lab and unpacked a shipment of drugs a delivery service had dropped off.

"They finally sent you that horse wormer you ordered," Kelly informed Erica.

"Good. Now I can pay George back what I borrowed from him."

"Do you want me to take it down there?"

"No," Erica answered, not noticing the eagerness in Kelly's voice. "I'll do it right after lunch."

The morning wore on. Only two other clients showed up. As Erica examined the bill from the drug company, she wondered how she would pay it. The bank account was running low, and there were other bills sitting on her desk waiting to be paid.

*   *   *

It had not been a good morning for Lyle Kline. Jewel, his wife was becoming impatient, and Kline's breakfast had been punctuated by her whining complaints. Why didn't he have this case wrapped up? Here it was, Thursday already. Had Schultz confessed? Why not? What was Lyle going to do about it?

As he approached the courthouse, he saw a big brown sheriff's car pull out and recognized Pete Torgeson in his broad-brimmed pearl gray Stetson at the wheel. When the sheriff made his daily progress through the town, he walked. He could meet more citizens that way. He would always stop, shake the hand of someone he knew, and engage in a few minute's conversation. That he was driving a car meant an errand out of town.

Kline sighed in relief. With the sheriff out of the way, he could have a free hand with Herb Schultz.

Kline ordered the jailer to bring Schultz to the interview room. Herb entered with a look of contempt on his face, dropped into the chair indicated, and reached into the breast pocket of the orange coveralls to pull out cigarette papers and tobacco.

"Put those away!" Kline ordered.

"This ain't never been a no-smokin' place," the prisoner replied, continuing his activity.

"I can't stand cigarette smoke," Kline complained.

Herb Schultz merely shrugged. He filled the paper with tobacco, tamping it down carefully in order to get more into the paper, rolled the cigarette and twisted the ends. He placed it in his mouth and dug into his pocket for a match.

"You can't smoke that in here," Kline shouted.

Herb furrowed his brow and stared at the lawyer. "You goin' to stop me?" He took the hand-rolled cigarette out of his mouth. A flake of tobacco clung to his lower lip and he stuck out his tongue to flick it off. He reached a work-roughened finger and thumb to his mouth and removed the flake of tobacco from the tip of his tongue. His eyes held a challenge.

Kline fumed, repeating his demand. But Herb diverted his attention to lighting his cigarette. Having found a large kitchen match in his pocket, he lit it by scraping a thumbnail across it. He held the flame to the end of the cigarette, inhaled deeply, then removed the fag from his mouth and exhaled a stream of smoke directly across the table into Kline's face. Kline jumped to his feet, coughing and waving his hands to steer the smoke away. He took a seat at the end of the table, away from the blue-gray vapor. He knew that if he called a deputy, he would only be told that prisoners were allowed to smoke.

Round one to Schultz.

Kline busily pulled materials from his briefcase, placed a pad in front of him and picked up a pen.

"Now, I want you to tell me exactly what you did on Saturday night," he said, trying to sound firm.

"I already told you that. I done went home and went to bed."

"No you didn't," Kline shouted. "Don't play games with me. We know you went down to Pettijohn's place."

"That was Sunday mornin'."

"No it wasn't and you know it!"

"Sure it was. I was down there when you come and arrested me."

"I don't mean *that* time. You know what I mean."

Herb shrugged and said nothing.

"You went down there Saturday night."

"Sunday mornin'. I done went there when I saw somethin' wrong. Then I was there again when you come."

"That's not how it happened and you know it."

"If you ain't goin' to listen to me, why ask me questions?"

"I don't want any of your smart backtalk."

"Well, you don't seem to learn real good. I told you what I done that mornin'."

"I'm not talking about Sunday morning! What happened on Saturday night?"

"I don't know nothin' about Saturday night. I was in bed. I done went right to sleep. I was drunk."

And Kline could not shake Herb on this simple statement.

Round two also to Herb.

And so it went; Kline made no headway and the old logger clung calmly to his story. Eventually Kline had to concede defeat and slink away.

*   *   *

Otis Vanderpool was in a much better mood. As his wife served him a stack of hotcakes with butter and maple syrup, he perused the accounts of the case in the Clarion.

"They're just making stuff up," he remarked. "We used to feed reporters little bits of information to chew on just so they wouldn't distort idle rumors all out of proportion."

"Pete Torgeson isn't saying anything, is he?"

"No, he isn't. And if I know Pete, that means he's not sure of his case and doesn't want to put a foot wrong. I'm delighted. It makes my job easier."

"You really think you can win this, don't you."

"I do. It has great possibilities."

Mrs. Vanderpool poured her husband another cup of coffee. "I don't see how you're going to get around those tracks, though."

"Oh, you just watch me," her husband gloated. "I'll do a regular dance around them."

"How?" she challenged.

"Herb was drunk when he left the Deerhorn. There are half a dozen witnesses to that."

"All of them drunk, themselves."

"Not all. The bartender wasn't. He is very experienced and can judge a man's state of inebriation with a great deal of accuracy. Herb had already reached the stumbling stage. Carl Nelson gave the excuse of wanting to get up the hill before it snowed too much, but he says his main reason in leaving early was to get Herb home while he was still able to navigate, when he could build up his fire, get undressed and in bed on his own. He figured that if Herb got any more inebriated, he'd pass out on the floor of his shack and freeze to death. Carl said he waited in the road long enough to see Herb's light come on and smoke start to come out of the chimney. That's why he didn't get any farther up the road to his trailer. There wasn't that much snow when they got to Herb's shack, but by the time Carl left there, a lot more had fallen."

"Was he there long enough to see whether Herb left again?"

"Herb didn't leave during the time it took Carl to get to his trailer. He would have noticed. But that doesn't mean anything. Herb made those tracks after the snow stopped. He says he made them in the morning. Kline says he did it later that night."

"What do *you* think?"

"Herb tells a straightforward story. It makes sense. It's perfectly logical. Now you try to fit Herb into Kline's scenario and you run into trouble."

"In what way?"

"When Herb made those tracks, he was using a long, steady stride and the line of tracks is straight as an arrow. I've seen the photos. Pete let me see them, though I'm sure Kline would have objected if he'd known. That Caldwell kid is a good photographer. He used the light and shadow to show the depth and crispness of the tracks. You can see the tread marks that Herb's boot soles made. There's no question that Herb made the tracks. He doesn't deny it. But I can't imagine that a drunk man, walking in the dark, carrying a rifle, could walk through deep snow in such a straight line, with such an even tread."

"Then how do you explain who shot Eugene Pettijohn if Herb made the tracks Sunday morning and Pettijohn was killed after it had snowed."

"My dear, *I* don't have to explain it. All I have to do is show a jury that Herb couldn't have."

"What about this theory that Herb took the milk pail that night and made up an excuse to milk the cow in the morning?"

"I can shoot all kinds of holes in that."

"How?"

"First and foremost, he had no way of knowing his dog would get sick. He had to have an excuse to walk down that road early on a frigid Sunday morning. He had one—one that was real. Erica Merrill confirmed that. She apparently told Kline off when he suggested that Herb made it up. She says the symptoms would not have started by Saturday night, but that they were real on Sunday morning.

"Second: tracks again. Straight, firm tracks leading to the barn. Not made by a drunk man stumbling around in the dark with a milk pail in one hand and a rifle in the other. Also, there is no mark anywhere that would indicate that a rifle was put down; not by the barn door and not by the gate. Herb would have to have held the rifle while he opened and closed them. It would be much more natural to lean it against the barn or the fence."

"You're really enjoying this case, aren't you dear?"

"As you say, I'm having a ball. I'm going to take young Lyle Kline over my knee and spank him."

CHAPTER 15

As Erica pulled into the parking lot of the Riverside Animal Clinic, she noted with rather smug satisfaction that there weren't many vehicles parked there. The ones that were present were farm trucks, indicating George's large animal clients. There were two people in the waiting room, one picking up medication for his cattle, the other asking for worm medicine for his farm dogs. Not exactly the flocks of clients anxious to see Trent, as he had led Erica to believe.

Perhaps, Erica thought, the slowness is mainly due to the weather.

She dropped off the equine wormer and thanked the receptionist for the loan of the drug. As she left, she decided that since she was in the area, she would drop in on Sarah Pettijohn. She could use as her excuse the need to determine the status of the cat, Orphan Annie (née Aphrodite), and to report on the health of the cow and calf.

About a hundred yards up the Boulder road from the highway, a road turned off to the right, crossed Boulder Creek, then turned left and followed the stream all the way back to town. Various farm lanes turned off from it. Erica took the first of these, and shortly found the driveway to Sarah's house. This was a relatively new structure, with yellow aluminum siding and white trim, set up against the base of the hill that led to Laird Bench. Erica could see why Sarah had wanted to get her car into the carport before too much snow had fallen. The driveway up to the carport was quite steep. Sarah's car was now in the carport and a sporty red Toyota with a Washington license plate stood in the parking area below the house. Erica parked beside it and climbed the steps to the front porch.

The door was opened by an attractive young woman with friendly hazel eyes and long red hair hanging in a ponytail over her shoulder. She gave Erica a smile, showing perfect white teeth, and said, "Hello. You want to see Sarah, don't you? Come in. I'll tell her you're here."

"Who is it?" Sarah called in her small voice from another room.

Erica responded, "It's Dr. Merrill, to report on Eugene's animals."

Sarah appeared in a doorway. "Come on in." To the girl she said, "Would you get Dr. Merrill a cup of coffee?"

"Sure. What do you take in it?"

"Nothing. Just black."

Erica removed her gloves and her parka and sat in the chair Sarah indicated. The girl returned with a steaming mug. Hammering could be heard in the background.

"This is my stepdaughter, Jennie," Sarah said. "She and her new hubby came over to Eugene's funeral."

"Oh yes. That was this morning, wasn't it?"

"Yes. Fortunately, he wasn't buried. I don't know how they'd have dug a grave in this weather! He was cremated. He asked to have his ashes scattered in the woods somewhere. Jennie has promised to come back next summer and do that."

"Are you Eugene's niece, then?" Erica asked.

"Yes. I'm Wilbur Pettijohn's daughter."

"I was Wilbur's second wife, you see," Sarah explained. "And, you know, the only thing good that has come out of this whole affair is that we've gotten acquainted with each other."

"Mom wouldn't let me meet Sarah. She hated her. And it isn't as if Sarah took Dad away from Mom. She didn't meet Dad until after the split. I wasn't even allowed to talk to her at Dad's funeral. I was only a teenager then, and Mom kept us strictly apart."

Sarah took up the tale, which both women seemed very pleased about. "But Jennie decided to come and meet me this time."

"That was Dan's idea. Dan's my husband. He said I ought to let bygones be bygones and come and see Sarah. Then I could decide for myself."

"I'm so glad she did. I missed having a daughter, even a step-daughter."

"Is that Dan banging away in there?" Erica asked.

"Yes," Jennie replied. "Hey, Dan. Come and meet the vet."

The hammering stopped. A tall young man with a mop of dark brown hair and a twinkle in his dark eyes appeared in the doorway.

Sarah said, "Dan's putting up some curtain rods for me. He's found all sorts of chores to do around the place. He shoveled out the whole driveway and all the walks and took the snow off the carport roof. I'm not sure I'll let them go back to Tacoma. Dan, get yourself a cup of coffee and join us. You need a rest. This is Dr. Merrill, our vet. She has Eugene's cat at her place, and she made sure the cow got milked."

"Glad to meet you." Dan strode across the room and extended a large hand, a smile lighting up his face.

Erica had expected doom and gloom, not this outpouring of friendly conviviality. But another thought entered her mind. She tried to slap it down, but it wouldn't go away.

Everyone had assumed that the motive for Eugene Pettijohn's death was one of a feud with a logger. Here was another motive. Money. Specifically inheritance. A nephew. A sister-in-law in whom he took a protective interest. Now a niece. *Hmmm!*

As if reading her mind, Sarah chattered on. "We had the reading of the will this morning after the funeral. We knew pretty well what the terms were. He told us some time ago. He gave ten percent to charity, ten percent to me and forty percent to Jennie and Ronnie. I didn't need anything, but we've been fairly close since Wilbur died. He left me well taken care of. He split everything between me and Jennie. He had some good investments and the store brought a lot when it was sold. He used to own the feed store, you know."

Erica nodded. "Yes, I remember him. You mean that Wilbur split his estate between you?"

"That's right. Well, when he died, we sold out to the AgriMaster chain. He also had insurance policies made out to both of us, Jennie and me, I mean."

Jennie interrupted the flow of words. "I used mine to go to the community college and learn bookkeeping. I figured there would always be a need for bookkeepers, especially since a lot of the older ones don't know the new computer programs. Then I figured that later I could go on and become an accountant."

"But then she met me," Dan said, smiling down at his wife.

"I got a job with the Toyota agency and made eyes at the boss' son." Jennie slipped her hand into Dan's and they exchanged loving looks. Well, that explained the fancy red sports car in the driveway.

"So it's Ronnie who needs the money," Erica suggested.

"Oh, no!" Sarah vociferated. "He has lots." Seeing Erica's raised eyebrows, she went on, "When his folks were killed in that car crash, they didn't have a will, so he inherited everything—about a hundred thousand dollars all together. Eugene had it put in a trust fund. He rather unwillingly agreed to take charge of him. I knew it wouldn't work, but he felt he had to. That was four years ago. Wilbur had already died, so he was his only close relative.

"Ronnie was a handful. His folks, Wilbur's and Eugene's sister, tried for years to have a baby. They'd given up, then much to their surprise, along he came. Well, they just spoiled him rotten. Then he came to live with Eugene, who never had any kids of his own. He tried to raise him like he'd been raised himself, real strict. He just couldn't handle him. Not that he's a bad kid, just wild and irresponsible."

"Eugene was also a perfectionist, as I recall," Erica mused. "He probably expected Ronnie to be as careful with things as he was."

"Boy you sure hit the nail on the head there!"

"I take it Ronnie isn't?" Jennie queried.

"You can say that again! Anyway, about that trust fund—Eugene felt he could support the two of them quite well on his income, so he put all of his money, Ronnie's money I mean, in a trust fund in a bank in Lincoln. He and the bank were trustees. He couldn't get it himself till he turned twenty one, but the trustees could have let him have some if he needed it for college or to start a business or get married or whatever."

"Did Ronnie know about this?"

"Oh, sure!"

Erica rubbed her chin. "Well, that solves one mystery," she stated pensively.

"What's that?"

"How he got Lolita Spillman to marry him."

"Oh, that girl! Eugene would have put a stop to that the next day. He wasn't old enough."

"Yes, but what I mean is that Lolita likes them with money. She always made eyes at the guys who came into the bar with big rolls of dough."

Sarah snorted. "Those guys! They had big wads when they cashed their paychecks, but they were broke before the next payday."

"Probably thanks in part to this girl you're talking about," Dan suggested.

"No doubt," Erica agreed. "But what I mean is that she wouldn't have looked at a penniless teenager, but if he told her he had a hundred thousand dollars in a trust fund and could get it if he got married…"

"I see what you mean," Jennie replied.

"But he still couldn't have gotten it unless the trustees said so," Sarah argued.

"He might not have told Lolita that."

"Oh! I see!"

"It just goes to show, there's usually a perfectly logical explanation for things if one knows all the facts."

Everyone nodded in agreement. There was a pause in the conversation, then Jennie remarked, "You know, I feel sorry for that boy. He's lost all his immediate family. At the funeral, I thought he looked sort of pasty-faced and he shivered all the time."

Erica decided she wouldn't say anything about Clay's account of how Walt Forgey had told the boy about his guardian's death. It was enough to make anyone pasty-faced.

"That's right. He sure didn't look good," Sarah agreed. "I guess he nearly passed out when they took him to the cabin to get some clothes. He's staying with that couple who run the jail. The man does the work in the jail and his wife cooks meals for the prisoners. They took him out to the cabin and they had to take him through the living room because his bedroom opened off of it. I guess they had to get him sat down on the floor with his head between his knees while they packed his stuff for him."

"Poor kid," Jennie said.

"What will happen to him now?" Erica asked.

"I don't know. He's not coming here, I'll tell you that."

"There must be some agency that takes care of minors."

"I suppose so."

"Anyway, I'd better talk to you about Eugene's animals before I forget. The cow is being taken care of. Clay Caldwell goes out every day to check on it." Erica decided to gloss over the problems. "The cat is doing well at our place. Sarah, I know you don't want it, but how about you, Jennie."

Jennie shook her head. "We have two Corgis and they don't like cats. Besides, I don't think I'd care for a Siamese. What will happen to her?"

"She gets along fine with my grandmother. We'll adopt her if that's okay with you."

"Oh, that's fine! That would be great if you'd do that."

"Done! Well, I'd better be going. Thanks for the coffee. And I'm so happy that you've found each other. As you said, one good thing came out of this affair."

But it was hard to imagine a loving reunion offsetting the reality of a brutal murder.

*   *   *

When Erica reached the road leading to Boulder along the south side of the creek, she turned right and followed it rather than going back to the highway. Being the old road to Boulder, it meandered with every bend in the creek. On the outskirts of town, it crossed an old wooden bridge that spanned Black Bear Creek at its junction with Boulder Creek. A youth in a four-wheel-drive sport utility vehicle roared past Erica about a half mile downstream from the bridge, and when Erica rounded the last curve, she saw the youth's vehicle slewed across the road, right in the middle of the bridge, its bumper locked with that of a pickup truck, the two machines completely blocking all traffic. A hulking farmer had the youth cornered between the truck and the bridge railing and was bending over him, shouting and gesticulating wildly.

I hope he doesn't throw him in the creek, Erica thought.

She could see that there would be no getting into town over this bridge for some time, so she put the Cherokee in reverse and backed about two hundred yards to the first plowed driveway where she could turn around. The thin wail of a siren could be heard from the direction of the river, so she waited in the driveway until the sheriff's Blazer had passed, its red and blue lights flashing. Walt Forgey was driving it. *Good*, thought Erica. She wanted to talk to Clay, to tell him what she had learned. If he'd been sent to the accident site, he'd have his mind on other things.

Erica drove back toward the river, crossed Boulder Creek and turned onto the main road. She made time into town. At the courthouse, she huffed and puffed up the flights of stairs to the third floor, her winter clothing a drag in the stuffy interior. Clay wasn't there. He had just gone out to check on the cow, then to interview some witnesses, the dispatcher told her.

Erica headed out of town and climbed onto Black Bear Ridge. As she parked beside Eugene Pettijohn's barn, she could see new tracks of Clay's pickup. He'd been and gone. Oh, well. She'd try him again later.

Then she remembered that this was the afternoon that Eddie Lee Dibble was to show up for "work." Oh, oh! She wondered what time the school had gotten out and whether Eddie Lee had arrived at her clinic to be greeted by a mystified Kelly.

It was a quarter to four. She turned the Jeep toward the clinic and hurried as fast as she dared. About two blocks away, she saw the boy, running as fast as he could in the snow, slipping and sliding as he went. She beeped her horn and pulled up beside him. He jumped the piled snow on the edge of the street and scrambled into the vehicle.

At the clinic, Kelly sat at her desk, making out vaccination reminder cards, her long, dark brown hair hanging down over the side of her face.

"Anything on for the rest of the afternoon?" Erica asked.

"No," Kelly replied sullenly. Not noticing the tone of the girl's reply, Erica explained Eddie Lee's presence, then went with him to the kennel to introduce him to the animals. As he made their acquaintance, Erica went back to the office.

Kelly continued her chore for a few more minutes, then pushed the pile of cards away and said, "There. Those are caught up to date. There weren't many."

"Thanks. You might as well go home."

"I should file these."

"You can do that tomorrow."

"The animals aren't fed."

"That's okay. I'll take care of them."

Kelly whirled around to face Erica. "Look! I need a full-time job. You keep sending me home early. I'm not getting many hours this week."

"I'm sorry. It's just the weather. When this cold spell breaks, people will come in again. Riverside is slow, too. There wasn't anything going on down there, either."

"That's not what Dr. Somers said. He said all your clients are going down there now."

"He's talking through his hat."

"Well, when I came to work here, it was supposed to be a full-time job. I wouldn't have taken the job if it wasn't."

"Kelly, I'm sorry that things are slow now. It can't be helped. I'll make it up to you some way when things pick up. But stay on until five today."

"Thanks."

"Feed Belle right away so we can take anything she doesn't eat away from her before we close up. Let her have water overnight. I'll come downstairs and take it away from her as soon as I get up in the morning."

"Okay. Anything else?"

"You might as well file those cards."

Erica went back to the kennel to find the boy stroking a large orange and white cat that had been boarding for over a week. The puss was delighted with the extra attention, arching his back and purring like a well-oiled engine.

"This cat's owners call him 'Motorboat' because of his purr."

Eddie Lee giggled. "He sounds like one. Hey, I'm sure glad you're letting me do this. I told my teacher I was coming here and she thought that was fine, cuz I need the extra stim…, uh, stimal…, uh…"

"Stimulus?"

"Yeah, that's it. Stim-u-lus." He tried it out a couple of times. "I'm supposed to write something about it for class on Monday."

"Good. That will be a good exercise. If you need any help spelling words, just let me know."

"Okay. I probably will. I don't spell too good."

"You should say, 'I don't spell too well.'"

"Oh." He tried that out until he had memorized it. Erica was getting to like the boy better and better.

"Let's feed the dogs and cats. There is a dog in the outside run that Kelly has already fed, but you can bring her in after she's eaten. Never go up to a dog when it's eating. It might bite you."

"My brothers won't let me go with them when they feed the dogs, 'cause they might bite me."

"I didn't think hounds were mean."

"Well, I guess these here hounds are." Eddie Lee's attention had been distracted from hounds to the sight of the Australian Shepherd, seen through the door when Kelly came back in from feeding her. "Oh! That's a pretty dog. Can I pet it?"

"Sure. She's friendly."

Eddie Lee bounded around the clinic, seeming fascinated by the array of equipment. He asked questions about everything. At home, he had been shy, but away from his family, he turned out to be a non-stop talker, and had a question about everything he saw. Erica had a hard time keeping up with him. As with Lena Lemm, she finally had to put her mind in neutral, as a flood of words inundated her. But like a log drifting downstream in a flood, one remark caught her attention instantly.

"I told them brothers of mine not to rob your place like they said they were going to."

"What?"

"I told them you were my friend so leave you alone."

"They didn't really say that, did they?"

"They asked me to case the joint." Eddie Lee giggled.

"I think they were just pulling your leg."

"Doing what?"

"Teasing you." *I hope so, anyway*, Erica thought.

"I guess maybe so. But anyway they promised not to rob you."

"That's nice of them."

"Yeah. I like my brothers."

"Anyway, there isn't anything here for them to steal. I don't keep money in the clinic, and the drugs are locked up. Besides there aren't enough drugs to be worth stealing."

"I'll tell them that."

"That's good, but Eddie Lee…"

"What?"

"If I were you, I wouldn't tell them you told me what they said."

"Oh! Okay." The boy giggled again.

"Seriously!"

"Okay. I gotcha."

From the parking lot, Erica could hear the sound of a horn. "That's probably your dad, so go get your coat and boots on."

As the boy squirmed into his coat, Erica poked her head out the door. A dark blue county pickup truck stood in the lot, its engine idling.

"He'll be out in a minute," Erica shouted.

Jess Dibble waved to indicate that he had heard.

"When should I come back? I can't come tomorrow. We're going on a field trip in the afternoon."

"Come Monday, then."

"Okay. I'll see ya." He dashed out the door.

Erica went into her office and shut the door. She dialed Clay's home number, but there was no answer.

CHAPTER 16

Wade and Heather stopped by the house for supper, which was a hasty affair so that they could get to the basketball tournament in Forks without missing too much of it. Wade had checked on the times of the games. The Forks Coyotes, being the host team, would play last, their opponents being the Fort McDonald Jackrabbits from Montana. Two teams from the state of Washington were matched in the first game of the evening.

It was dark in the canyon as they followed the Whitewater River down to the point where it met a large tributary stream, giving the little town of Forks its name. They could not see the river, but knew it was there, dark and menacing, frozen over in patches, but with rapids throwing cascades of spray over the rocky shore, encasing everything within reach in a sheet of ice. There was black ice on the highway, and Wade steered the big four-door pickup truck carefully, knowing the road, knowing where to expect the ice.

Forks was ablaze with light, cars and pickups converging on the school. Excited shouts reverberated from the gym, where the first game was already in progress. They paid the admission fee and had their hands stamped with ink to show they had paid, in case they wanted to go out for a breather between the games. The stands were filling up. They found seats about half way up.

The style of play of the Indian teams was predicated on offense, with intense end-to-end action. Defense was minimal, fouls were few and unintentional, the pace swift. There were only a few really tall players, and none over about six feet three or four. When one player accidentally knocked an opponent down, he reached down to help the man back to his feet and the two trotted down the court grinning and talking to each other. Since most of the crowd was neutral they cheered both teams indiscriminately, applauding difficult shots that found their mark and groaning at ones that missed. The game was tied at halftime.

Erica knew a few of the spectators and waved at them when she caught their eye. Occasionally one would stop for a few words. Most were Indians, but a few local whites had showed up. The atmosphere was festive and gregarious.

"Its a lot different than high school games, isn't it?" Heather remarked.

"Yes, a lot more fun," Erica replied leaning across Wade, who sat between them, and shouting to make herself heard over the din. "You'll never hear anyone boo—not even at the refs."

"You hardly notice the referees. They don't seem to have much to do."

Wade nodded. "These fellows could play this entire game without a ref, actually. They would even agree on fouls. They know the rules and play by them."

"Sport the way sport should be," Heather declared.

"Absolutely."

Erica picked up the thread. "And no one sitting behind the backboards trying to distract players from hitting free throws."

"Erica, do you remember that time when Coach threatened to pull the football team off the field if the crowd didn't behave themselves?"

Erica groaned. "I sure do!"

Wade turned to Heather. "It was during our state championship season. The fans, mostly the parents, were being thoroughly obnoxious to the visiting team, using language that would blister your ears. Coach didn't think that was appropriate at a high school game, so during a time out, he called us off the field to the bench, then he turned to the crowd and bellowed until he got their attention, then told them he'd pull us off the field for good if they didn't behave themselves. That would mean forfeiting the game, which would have put us out of the playoffs. You could have heard a twig snap! We went back out there and won the game, with the crowd cheering for us but not saying another dirty word about the other team."

"He must have been quite a guy."

"He was. We haven't had a coach since who could hold a candle to him."

"Clay quit the team the next year," Erica remarked. "He couldn't stand the new coach."

"Yeah. That guy made it a sort of boot camp type atmosphere. That's not the thing to do with high school kids. In fact, a lot of them aren't really that keen on the game, but in a small town, any boy who is big or who is tall gets pressured into playing football or basketball. Treating them like a bunch of military recruits just isn't right."

The teams ran back onto the court for a brief warm-up before the second half. A small girl who appeared to be about three years old, had toddled out onto the floor, surveying the crowd with interest. The leading player of one of the teams scooped her up and holding the giggling child high over his head, walked along the stands until her smiling mother extricated herself from the crush of spectators and claimed her.

Heather remarked, "I've noticed that all the adults seem to feel responsible for all the children. I'm so used to adults ignoring other people's children for fear of offending the parents."

"That's right," Erica answered her. "It used to be this way in all small towns. Dad tells of being scolded by other adults when he was a child. He said it was harder for kids to get in trouble then because everyone was watching over them."

"I wonder how true that really is. I bet that if kids really wanted to get into mischief, they'd find a way."

"Probably so."

The game ended with a very close score, 122 to 118, making accurate Wade's prediction that the average score in these games was around 120. Toward the end of the game, the players for the next one made their way out of the locker room to watch the action. Erica spotted Charlie Oliver in his white uniform with the green and gold trim. He wore number 7, and Erica hoped it brought him luck. She watched him as he found a place to sit. He carefully wrapped his ankles and laced his high-topped shoes. Then as the first game ended and his team took the floor to warm up, he stood, did a bit of running in place, jumped a couple of times, landing on his toes, then raced onto the floor, took a bounce pass from a teammate and soared through the air toward the basket. With a lithe grace he effortlessly let go a soft shot that banked off the backboard and swished through the hoop.

Heather gasped. "He's like a beautiful horse!"

Wade nodded, and Erica marveled at the fitting description, though the animal that came to her mind was a deer. Charlie, she was sure, would not mind being compared to a horse or to a deer. She wondered if he had an Indian name, based upon some wild creature. Or had these modern natives gotten away from that?

Charlie did not start. About five minutes into the game, with the Coyotes trailing by six points, he came off the bench and immediately made an impact. In the next few minutes, during which the Coyotes scored ten points to the Jackrabbits' two, Charlie hit on two high, arcing jump shots that dropped through the mesh without touching the rim, and followed with a lay-in on a fast break. The Coyotes took their first lead of the game. He played the rest of the half.

The Coyotes trotted off to the locker room at half-time leading by two points, 62 to 60. Erica watched Charlie disappear through the doorway, glanced up at the scoreboard, then with a jolt saw Charlie standing right in front of her! But of course it wasn't Charlie, it was Louie. He greeted Wade, was introduced to Heather, then turned his attention to Erica.

"I heard you wanted to talk to Charlie," he said with a frown.

"I'd like to if he has time after the game."

"Look. Charlie's a good kid. I don't want him getting into any trouble. He wasn't really hanging around with that group of kids that Ronnie Bixby runs with. He doesn't care much for them."

"I know. And that's exactly the point. I'd like to put this rumor to rest that he was part of a group going around with a gun the night Eugene was shot. I want to know exactly what happened."

Louie looked pensive, the frown still showing on his face.

"You know, don't you," Erica continued persuasively, "that one of Cliff Bodine's former deputies is trying to blame the shooting on him. I don't think anyone else believes it, but I'd like to get it cleared up."

"Well, I guess…"

"It's all right, Louie," Wade said. "It won't harm him."

"Okay, Wade, if you say so." A glance passed between the two men that made Erica envious of the close relationship that can be built up between men who have been through difficult experiences together. Wade and Louie and Clay and Bill Clarke. Whenever they were together, others might as well be on another planet. Would she ever have a relationship like that—one of trust and respect based on understanding the other's needs and knowing what made them tick?

As Louie turned to leave, Heather called after him, "Good luck to Charlie in the second half."

Louie turned, the frown replaced by a broad grin. "Those Coyotes are going to feast on Jackrabbits tonight!"

*   *   *

The Jackrabbits gave them a run for it, though. They hit a bucket to break a tie with only seconds to go. A teammate inbounded the ball to Charlie who caught it on the dead run, dribbled once then let go one of his high, overhand shots. It hit the rim and bounced straight up, and as the buzzer sounded, it seemed to hang agonizingly in mid-air before dropping straight through the hoop. The game was tied.

But the Coyotes went to work in overtime, building up a five point lead and holding onto it. They won by a score of 138 - 133. The building erupted in celebration.

It wasn't long after the game before Charlie and Louie appeared, making their way through the departing crowd to where the three Merrills were still seated. Charlie appeared relaxed and happy, and everyone congratulated him on a great game. He had scored twenty-one points, not bad for a debut! They chattered away about the game until the subject had been exhausted. Then Charlie said to Erica, "My brother says you want to know about Saturday night."

"That's right. What can you tell us?"

"I don't ordinarily hang out with that crowd."

"We know that."

"But Saturday night, I saw Ronnie and a couple other guys and they had this rifle. I could see that it was a lever-action thirty-thirty, and Louie had told me about Eugene's gun, so I thought that if that's the one Ronnie had, I'd like to see it."

"I'd told Charlie and my Dad and sister about it," Louie explained. "It was a couple years ago. Eugene had Dad make him a bolo tie, and I took it out to Eugene's place to show it to him to see if it was the way he wanted it made. Dad doesn't get around much, you know."

Erica nodded and Louie went on. "I saw this rifle on the rack above the fireplace and I said something about it. Eugene took it down and showed it to me, and if you knew that guy you'd know that you didn't ask him a question unless you really wanted to know the answer. He gave me the entire history, not only of that model of rifle but of that particular gun as well. He even told me about how the town of Winchester got its name — from the name of the gun that everybody owned."

They all nodded and waited for Louie to continue.

"That was the most beautiful gun I ever saw. It had a deer jumping a log etched on one side of the action, and an elk with a mountain and forest background on the other. There was a deer's head carved on one side of the stock and an elk's head carved on the other side. He kept it in perfect condition."

"Yeah, and ever since Louie told us about it, I wanted to see it. So there was Ronnie with this gun, and I just went across the street to take a look at it. It sure was pretty, just like Louie said."

"What was Ronnie doing with it?"

"Just showing it off. Then this other kid said he'd swiped a shell from his dad's box when he was unloading his rifle last fall when he came back from hunting. And he pulled it out of his pocket and said, 'Let's go shoot it.' Well, that's when I checked out. That Ronnie isn't too careful where he points a gun, so if he had ammo for it, I didn't want to be anywhere around."

"Was it the right caliber — a thirty-thirty?"

"I don't know. I didn't stick around to see."

Wade asked, "Was it a rimmed cartridge? If it was, it was probably a thirty-thirty. If it was rimless, it may have been a thirty-ought-six and they couldn't have shot it anyway."

Charlie shook his head. "I beat it," he said.

"Good for you."

"Do you know where they went after that," Erica asked.

"They said something about going out to the rifle range."

"Did Ronnie load the gun before they left?"

"I didn't see, but I expect so — if the shell was the right size. That Ronnie wouldn't be caught dead walking around with an unloaded gun!"

*   *   *

The three Merrills made their way out into the night. Most of the other vehicles had left already and they found themselves in the dark parking lot looking at a clear black sky filled with stars. Millions of them. The Milky Way stood out as if a handful of dust had been carelessly tossed across the sky. They stood beside the truck for a long moment drinking in the beauty of the night. The cold caught their breath and congealed it in front of their faces, and eventually caused them to abandon their vigil and seek the shelter of the truck's interior. It took a while for the heater to dispel the cold, and as they drove north along the river, they reviewed Charlie's story.

Wade summed it up. "I hope that ex-deputy doesn't try to stir up a lot of trouble for Charlie. Like Louie said, he's a nice kid."

CHAPTER 17

For Clay Caldwell, Thursday evening had been neither as exciting nor as productive. It seemed he was destined to interview all the witnesses who were unwilling to talk and couldn't readily be compelled to do so. The one who seemed anxious to help had information that was probably worthless.

Clay spent nearly an hour trying to track down the two boys who had been seen with Ronnie Bixby. They weren't at either of their homes. They had left the school, not having any extracurricular activities to occupy them, and they weren't in the usual teen-age haunts. He finally found them in the supermarket. He waited until they had paid for their soft drinks and potato chips, and caught them as they left the store.

It appeared that they were deaf, blind and dumb. Especially dumb — in either sense of the word.

They couldn't remember whether they had been with Ronnie on Saturday. They saw him every once in a while, but they didn't keep track of when it was. They didn't remember a gun. Hadn't Ronnie showed them his uncle's rifle. They exchanged vague glances, then shrugged. When pressed, they recalled that at some time he had shown them a rifle, but they couldn't remember when. A while ago, was all he could get out of them. Did they by any chance make plans with him to shoot the Winchester? They shook their heads. When did they part from Ronnie Saturday evening? Saturday? Who says they were with him Saturday?

Finally Clay gave up. Without authority to haul them off to the office and interrogate them until they decided to cooperate, he could accomplish nothing.

The Dibble boys weren't home either. Clay wanted to know where they had driven off to on Saturday night and why they were being so secretive about it.

Finally, he dropped into Mabel's Bar and Grill. Mabel greeted him with a sour visage.

"Are you here to eat, or do you want to give Lolita a bad time?"

"Both. But I won't be hard on her. I just want some information."

"Eat first, then. She's busy now."

"Okay. But make sure she doesn't take off out the back door."

"None of your sass! I need her here. She'll still be around when you're done eating. What do you want?"

"Some chili would taste fine right now."

"One bowl of chili coming up. You want coffee?"

"Yes, please."

Clay found a booth and wrapped his hands around the coffee mug while he waited for his food. Lolita was the one who served it, but she plunked the bowl of chili and a plate of bread and butter onto the table and shied away like a skittish horse. He was starting to eat when the old ex-deputy sauntered into the bar, and seeing Clay, wandered over.

"Have ya found that there Injun kid yet and hauled him in for questioning?"

"No."

"Well, ya oughtta. That right?" he asked the assembled barflies.

"Yeah. That's right, man," they chorused.

Clay decided to ignore the man and concentrate on his food until he heard Mabel bellow, "Get out! Out, you two." He jerked his head up in time to see the Dibble boys standing in the door, startled expressions on their countenances. They spotted him, turned irresolutely and shuffled out. He wanted to talk to them, but they would be long gone by the time he had a chance to get away. He was certain that they frequented this bar and were usually welcome, but the one time he wished they would stay, his very presence had chased them out.

"We don't allow no minors in this bar," Mabel shouted at their departing backs.

Perhaps it was just as well, the way things turned out, he reasoned. If he had arrived to find an underage youth being served, he would have been duty bound to take official action, especially as he was still in uniform, and would have lost his opportunity to talk to Lolita Spillman.

While he ate, the hot chili warming his insides, a man who was a stranger to him bustled over to the booth and introduced himself.

"You're working on the Pettijohn case, aren't you?"

"Yes."

"I can tell you where Pettijohn was in the early part of Saturday evening." The man seemed anxious to impart his information.

"Sit down. What do you know?"

"I have a tree farm out the Boulder Creek road. Pettijohn came to my house Saturday to discuss it with me; tell me how to manage it."

"Do you live out there?"

"No. I live here in town."

"What time was this?"

"He came at seven. He was there about an hour. Maybe a bit longer."

"Do you know whether he had any other appointments?"

"I don't think so. I think he went on home. You see, I work regular hours, so I had to ask him to come in the evening."

"Then this was an appointment set up ahead of time."

"Yes, it was. About a week ahead."

"All right. Thanks for the information." Clay jotted down the man's name, address and phone number, then returned to his meal.

One cooperative witness, at least, but one with information that had no real value to Clay. Eugene would have been home by eight thirty. No big deal.

He finished his chili and a second cup of coffee, left enough money to cover the bill and a tip on the table and caught Mabel's eye. He gave an almost imperceptible jerk of his head toward the kitchen and Mabel nodded. The ex-deputy had his back turned and stood in a knot of men laughing over some joke, probably a dirty one. Clay slipped hastily into the back room.

Lolita was surly and uncooperative. Clay apologized for the rough way she and Ronnie had been rousted out of bed on Sunday morning. Clay found that more and more it was necessary to smooth things over after Walt Forgey had riled people up. Clay assured Lolita that he only wanted some information about Ronnie's movements in order to complete a schedule of activity at the Pettijohn cabin on Saturday night. Lolita wasn't listening.

"I don't have anything to tell you cops," she snarled. "Get out of my hair!"

"In a few minutes," Clay responded quietly. "I don't want to inconvenience you."

"Then quit doing it!"

"Lolita, give me a break. I don't want to make any trouble for you. Or for Ronnie."

"Oh, him!" The girl's voice dripped with venom. "He can take care of himself for all I care."

"Just tell me what time he came down here on Saturday night."

"I don't know. Before I went off work."

"Ten? Ten fifteen?"

She shrugged. "I didn't look at the clock. He was here awhile before I went off at ten thirty."

"And he asked you to marry him at that time?"

"Yeah, so what?"

Only that he wasn't old enough to marry, that's all, Clay thought.

"Why did you agree to marry him on such short notice?"

"Why not?"

"I'm still asking you why."

"I thought he was a nice kid."

"But you don't now?"

"Now I think he's a louse. He wasn't even old enough."

"Didn't you know that?"

"How would I know?"

"Well, he was only a sophomore in high school."

"I don't keep track of anyone's school records."

"No other reason than that you thought he was a nice kid?"

"Isn't that enough?"

It wouldn't be for me, thought Clay, *and I doubt if it was for her.*

"Look, I've got work to do, Mr. Deputy Sheriff. So why don't you clear out and let me do it. I don't know anything."

Again, Clay had to admit defeat. He went out through the back door and trudged around to the parking lot where he'd left his pickup. He drove home. As he unlocked the door to his apartment, he could hear the phone ringing, but by the time he got to it, the caller had hung up.

*   *   *

Not being able to find Clay the previous evening before she left for the basketball tournament, Erica decided to get up early and drop into the sheriff's office before starting her day at the clinic. She had been told that Clay would come on duty at 7 AM. Bubbling over with the desire to impart her various bits of information, she had not slept well. She kept rolling the various threads of her investigation over in her mind, but could not make much of them. At least, she had some concrete information for Clay. She wondered what he might have dug up.

She resolutely kept her mind off the subject of tracks in the snow. That was technical stuff. Clay would have to work on that. If only he would approach the subject with an open mind, that he would look for some other explanation than the obvious one that since Herb Schultz had made the tracks, he must have killed Eugene Pettijohn.

Erica had no real interest in Herb Schultz. For that matter, she was aware that she was not motivated by any altruistic idea of seeing justice done. Her reasons were simple and she realized as much.

She would like to see Lyle Kline resoundingly defeated.

She did not want Clay to fall down on his first big case. She knew that many people in Mountain County thought that hiring a forensic expert was a waste of time and money, even though he did other police work as well. The old methods had always worked — or so people thought — so why bother with expensive new ones? She hoped that Pete Torgeson's confidence in his young deputy would be vindicated. If not, it could cost both of them their jobs.

And she wanted to be proven correct so that the local populace would have some respect for her judgment.

* * *

Clay found the interview room empty. Obviously Lyle Kline did not believe in getting to work at 7 AM to question his prisoner. Clay knew that Kline had not given up on that approach, and that Schultz had not changed his story, regarding the prosecutor with unveiled contempt. Spreading his evidence on the table, Clay set to work organizing it and reviewing the entire case in his mind. Perhaps if he had everything in front of him, something that had eluded him so far would pop up. After spending some time arranging his notes, photos and exhibits, he decided to start with the pictures.

He had taken panoramic shots of the Pettijohn property, and had even added a surveyor's map, which also showed the adjacent property of Herb Schultz, and of Lena Lemm, Carl Nelson and Jess Dibble across the road. Below the Pettijohn place, uninhabited woodland stretched to the end of the ridge and down the steep hillside. The Dibble place was across from this wood, Lena Lemm's property across from Eugene Pettijohn's, and Carl Nelson's across from Schultz's.

All these neighbors owned 30.30 rifles, the Dibbles possessing a veritable arsenal of weapons, a fact that made Clay nervous. They really had no need for all those guns, and Jess wasn't a collector like a couple of other men in this town. He knew they hunted; nearly everyone did. Jess also hunted cougar for bounty. He supposed that each of the three older sons had been given rifles as gifts, but thought that Zack and Cody should only be owning twenty-twos, not powerful hunting rifles. If there were also assault rifles, they were not on display. Nor did they go in for handguns, though Clay thought he had once seen Jess with a .357 Magnum.

Clay had taken a view of the cabin from the road. He had gotten this before all the traffic arrived. When he had gotten to the cabin, he had been careful to leave the gate and the front door exactly as he found them and had avoided obliterating any of Herb Schultz's footprints. Herb had walked down the road from the barn. From the barn? Well, maybe. He couldn't be sure because the snowplow had been by. But a set of tracks leading from the barn turned down the road toward the cabin. Another set turned up the road toward Schultz's shack. This was clear even though further tracks in either direction had been covered by the snow piled at the side of the road by the plow.

Did that fit into their concept of how the crime was committed? Schultz had supposedly gone down to

Pettijohn's cabin Saturday night after the snow had quit, then had gone out the back door to the barn, carrying the milk pail. From the barn he would have gone out to the road and back to his shack. In the morning, he would have gone down to the barn to milk the cow. Were there tracks turning in toward the barn from up the road? Yes, here they were. But they didn't go directly to the barn. They turned off the road and stopped. At that spot Schultz had halted and tramped around a bit before going in. Why?

The same thing had happened in front of the house. Schultz had stood outside the gate milling about before he had gone up the walk. That could probably be explained by his indecision as to whether to go on with his scheme. When he had gone in, his steps were firm and straight.

Back to the tracks by the barn. From the gate to the barn door, Schultz had walked back and forth in his tracks. The last set were from the barn to the gate. Here the tracks became muddled, and the gate itself had destroyed some as it moved the snow when it was opened and closed. Clay could not tell whether this last set of tracks connected with ones going up or down the road.

He went over in his mind the likely possibilities. Saturday night, after shooting Pettijohn, Schultz had taken the milk pail to the barn to be used in the morning. Then he had gone from the barn to the road. Where then? Hastily up to his shack? That seemed most likely. But might he have gone back down toward the cabin? What for? Would someone who had planned all this so carefully make the mistake of going back down the road and ruining the whole scheme? Could a man like Schultz have done all this planning? Suppose he had. Might he have been stupid enough to undo the whole scheme by making an extra set of tracks down the road? He couldn't count on the snowplow covering them up. Someone might have discovered the murder before the plow came along.

In fact, someone might have heard the shot and come to investigate or call the sheriff. Why didn't anyone hear the shot? Or were they covering up, or not wanting to get involved. In the clear crisp coldness of the night, when folks were in bed, their TV sets and radios off, the shot must have resounded very distinctly across the landscape. Earlier in the evening, or during the storm it might not have been heard. Did everyone around there sleep that soundly?

Back to the prints. Let's say Schultz went back to his shack, by whatever route. In the morning, he goes down the road to the barn. Why does he stop and mill about before he goes in? To see if anyone is looking? Why would that matter? But that won't work anyway because the tracks where he moved about in one spot all point toward the barn; they don't turn around. It looks as if he was trying to make up his mind about something, but why the hesitation?

Back off a bit, Clay told himself. Go back to the methodical examination of the pictures.

He had taken views of the tracks leading to the cabin as a whole and then of every individual one. He had examined them so often he had them memorized. The same with those leading from the cabin to the barn. He had searched all around the cabin for any other tracks. There were none. One set in. One set out. That was it.

The argument that Otis Vanderpool had advanced to his wife had also occurred to Clay. Could a drunk man, in the dead of night, carrying a rifle, and later a rifle and a pail, have made that straight, firm line of tracks? It hardly seemed likely.

Was Schultz really drunk? Could he have been shamming? Carl Nelson might know. They had been together all evening. Would Nelson cover up for Schultz? For that matter, could they have been in it together? Nelson's 30.30 was spotlessly clean. It could have been fired that night. But there was a hitch. Tracks again. Nelson had gone to his trailer before the snow had stopped falling. He had come out only once after that, to come down to the murder scene when he saw police cars congregating. How had the gun gotten back to Nelson's trailer?

There was also the fact that at no time had Schultz set a rifle down in the snow. The butt of the stock would have made a distinctive impression. He had set down the milk pail to open and close the barn door and the farmyard gate. On the way into the barn, the impression of the smooth bottom of the stainless steel bucket had been shallow. It was empty then, and cold. When Schultz had come out of the barn, he had set down the bucket, then filled with warm milk, and it had made a deeper, more definite impression in the snow. Ditto at the gate. He had set it down to open the gate and again to close it.

At none of these times did he put down a rifle. It didn't make sense.

Unless he had one with a sling. But slings weren't very common any more. Clay knew a few men who had them on their guns, but none of these were likely.

Maybe he'd left the rifle in the cabin and taken it out in the morning. No, that wouldn't work, because the idea was that he didn't go into the cabin in the morning, and Clay knew definitely that the only large caliber rifle in that cabin was the one hanging on the rack over the fireplace. Try as he might, he could not imagine Schultz getting possession of that gun, taking it to the other side of the room, shooting an unsuspecting Eugene Pettijohn, cleaning the gun and putting it back on the rack.

There was one possibility they had not yet considered; that had to do with the phone call. Sarah was adamant that Eugene had called her at ten o'clock as he always did. But what if there had not been a phone call? Then Eugene could have been killed before it snowed. Surely Sarah would have remembered if Eugene had not called, and there would have been no business about having to end the call early in order to get the car into the carport. Could Sarah be lying?

As hard as he might try, Clay could not visualize Sarah Pettijohn taking Eugene's rifle, which she had at her house, finding some ammo somewhere, and going out to shoot her brother-in-law. No that wouldn't work anyway. If Sarah had bought ammo for that gun, whoever she had bought it from would most certainly have remembered selling it to her. And besides, the gun wasn't at her house. Ronnie had it.

Could Sarah have been in league with someone else? If so, who? Herb? Ronnie? Nelson? Lena Lemm? The Dibbles? Every one of these pairs seemed unimaginable. Clay scouted the idea of Sarah's involvement as preposterous.

Clay began to seriously question his ability to solve the puzzles in this case. He needed to succeed, for the sake of his own career and for that of his friend, the sheriff, Pete Torgeson.

I've got to find something *that lets me get a handle on this case, he thought.* He went back with feverish haste to his assembled evidence.

CHAPTER 18

"Hi!"

Clay reluctantly shifted his focus from his display of evidence to the door of the room. There stood Erica, with an enigmatic smile that told him she was feeling pleased with herself. Now, what did she want?

"May I come in, or is all this super-secret?" she inquired, gesturing toward the table covered with evidence from the case.

"Actually, I shouldn't be showing this stuff to you."

"I shall avert my eyes, while you surreptitiously conceal any classified documents. Furthermore, I shall sit over here on this bench where I can't see anything anyway."

The bench actually appeared marginally more comfortable than the straight-backed chairs. She sat on it sideways, pulling her feet up onto the seat and wrapping her arms around her knees.

"What do you want," Clay asked, suspiciously.

"I have a couple of pieces of information for you."

Clay frowned. He was not comfortable with her butting in. She had no business talking to the witnesses, he thought, and she had gotten him in trouble with his boss. Yet, he couldn't exactly tell her to get lost. She might have some information that he needed.

"What sort of information?"

"I can tell you why Lolita agreed to marry Ronnie, for one."

She saw the consternation on his face and smiled. She waited.

"How do you know that? I just talked to Lolita last night and she wouldn't give me the time of day."

"You talked to the wrong person."

"So who was the right one then?"

"Sarah Pettijohn."

"Sarah! She doesn't know anything about Lolita."

"Right. But she knows an awful lot about Ronnie."

"Like what?"

"Like Ronnie's money."

"Ronnie doesn't have money. Granted Eugene was fairly well off, but he kept the kid on a pretty austere allowance."

"I mean Ronnie's own money."

"Come off it! That kid?"

Erica nodded.

"Oh, I get it. He will inherit from Eugene. But why tell Lolita that, and why would she think she could get her hands on it with Eugene still alive? He wouldn't have told her Eugene was dead, even if he knew. If Ronnie knew, he either killed his uncle and didn't want to be found out, or else he would have called us."

"Yes, he will inherit forty percent of Eugene's estate, but he already had money. In fact, by Boulder standards, he was comparatively rich. When his parents were killed, four years ago, he inherited their whole estate, around a hundred thousand dollars. Eugene invested the entire amount in a trust fund for Ronnie. By now, it's probably quite a bit larger."

She watched the stunned expression on Clay's face, then went on, "Eugene and the bank were trustees of the fund. Ronnie can't get hold of it on his own until he turns twenty-one. But the trustees can dole out money from it at their discretion—for college, or a business, or marriage. I'll bet you anything that dear little Ronnie told Lolita that if he got married, he could cash in on the trust fund."

"Did he know about it?" Clay asked weakly.

"Oh yes!"

Clay digested the information silently. Erica continued, "A lot of these loggers come into the bar flashing a big roll, but Lolita knows full well that it is easy come, easy go with them. But a hundred thousand dollars in the bank would be something else. Enough to cause a gold-digger like her to rob the cradle and agree to marry a teenager."

In the silence that followed, Pete Torgeson's voice could be heard in the outer office. Clay leapt to his feet and strode to the door.

"Hey, Pete. Come in here. I want you to hear this."

The sheriff entered the room, coffee cup in hand and a quizzical expression on his cold-reddened face. Seeing Erica, he tipped his Stetson.

"Good morning, Dr. Merrill."

She laughed. "Cut it out! I was mad when I told you to call me that."

"You sure were! What is it that I should hear?"

Clay nodded toward Erica, so she recounted the information about Ronnie's trust fund.

"Well, I'll be damned!" the sheriff exclaimed. "Just like that! So simple."

"I was thinking the same thing. People's actions often seem pretty logical when you know all the details."

Clay stirred. "You said Ronnie would inherit forty percent of Eugene's estate. Who gets the other sixty percent?"

"He left ten percent to charity, ten percent to Sarah, and forty percent each to his nephew and his niece."

"Niece?" the two men asked in unison.

"Wilbur Pettijohn's daughter by his first wife. Her name is Jennie. I didn't get her last name. She's married, quite recently, I would say." Erica went on to recount her entire conversation with Sarah and Jennie.

"I'll be damned!" The sheriff dropped into a chair. "I expect we'd better go talk to them. You know, concentrating on Schultz has put us off our normal routine. We should have known about all this stuff."

Clay nodded. Pete Torgeson glanced at Erica. "But don't tell anyone we said so!"

"Not a word!" Erica held up her hand as if being sworn.

Clay turned toward Erica. "You said you had some other information."

"Yes. It's about the kids Ronnie was hanging out with on Saturday night."

"So you talked to Charlie Oliver?"

"I did. He's a nice boy, and he sure can play basketball."

"How'd the game go?"

"Forks won it in overtime." She told Clay about Charlie's last second jump shot to tie the game.

"That team they beat was favored to win the tournament," Clay mused. "They have some really good players according to Louie. So if Forks beat them, they look good for the championship."

"We talked to Louie, also. He's very protective toward Charlie."

"Yeah. He does a pretty good job for a big brother who has to act like a father. So what did Charlie say?"

"He told us he saw Ronnie showing off the gun and wanted to see it himself. Louie had told him about it. Louie had seen the gun at Eugene's when he delivered something there. Eugene showed him the rifle and described its history. Louie told the other members of his family, so when Charlie saw Ronnie with a rifle, he thought it was probably that one and wanted to see it."

"I take it that it *was* that gun," Torgeson commented.

"Yes it was. But Ronnie and the other boys started talking about shooting it. Apparently one boy said he had

filched a cartridge from his father's box while his father was
unloading a rifle after coming home from hunting."

"A 30.30?"

"Charlie didn't know. He couldn't remember, or
hadn't noticed, whether it was a rimmed or rimless shell."

"I wonder what caliber gun the boy's dad shoots. We
know him, by the way."

"His dad shoots a two-seventy." They turned to see
Walt Forgey lounging in the doorway, coffee mug in hand.
"But his uncle has a 30.30 and his wife doesn't like guns in
the house, so he might have unloaded it at the other guy's
house."

Clay grimaced. "Why couldn't they unload their guns
out in the woods before they brought them home?"

Walt shrugged. "You can't tell guys like that
anything. They probably just always did it that way."

"Yeah," said Torgeson. "And at least once a year we
get somebody killed for exactly that reason. And a few more
with the shit scared out of them."

Clay returned to the subject at hand. "So Ronnie had
the rifle and possibly a shell that fit it. What then?"

"Charlie decided to leave. He doesn't trust Ronnie
with a loaded gun."

"Ronnie did load it then?"

"Charlie didn't know. He didn't wait around to find
out, but he was sure that if the shell fit, Ronnie would have
loaded it into the rifle. He heard them saying something
about going out to the rifle range and shooting it."

"They couldn't have. It's been locked up since the
end of hunting season."

"They might have found something else to shoot at.
The light over the gate, maybe."

"Then they missed," Walt stated as he slurped a
mouthful of coffee. "That light was still on when I came
down the hill on Sunday morning. I remember how it
reflected off the snow."

Clay ran his fingers through his hair. "They might not have found anything to shoot at, or the shell may have been the wrong size. Anyway, whether they shot it or not, Ronnie took it home before Eugene got home at about eight-thirty, left it on the rack and went out again."

"But he did shoot it," Erica insisted

"How do you figure that?"

"He had to clean it."

Clay hit his forehead with the heel of his hand as if to knock some sense into his brain. Pete Torgeson threw back his head and let out a great guffaw. "Erica, you ought to be on the force! How'd you like a badge?"

"Okay. When do I start?" She grinned at Torgeson, knowing it was a joke, but half wishing it wasn't. Her other occupation didn't seem to be paying her much these days.

"Let's get the events of the evening as we know them, or can surmise, straightened out," Clay suggested. "First, Ronnie went to get the gun. What time was that, Pete?"

"Sarah didn't remember exactly. She said about five-thirty or six."

"Probably five-thirty, because several people saw Ronnie and those other kids with it at six. Does that fit with what Charlie Oliver said?"

"I didn't ask," Erica replied. She made a face. "Sorry."

"It doesn't matter. So shortly after six, they head toward the rifle range, probably in Ronnie's heap. It's locked up, but they find something to shoot at. Then they go to the cabin, or Ronnie lets the other boys off in town and goes home. Eugene was out for a while in the early evening. He had an appointment with a man here in town to discuss a tree farm. He got there at seven and left not long after eight. He probably got home by eight thirty. Presumably, Ronnie had been and gone while Eugene was out, or Eugene would have made him do a good job of cleaning the gun."

"I wonder why Eugene didn't notice it?" Torgeson pondered. "He apparently went about his normal evening routine without noticing the gun with oil dripping off it."

"He probably noticed," Erica remarked. "I expect he was going to confront Ronnie with it the next day and make him do it right."

"Or later that night."

"No. Not that night."

"What makes you think that?"

"Because he didn't have his teeth in his mouth."

She heard Walt Forgey snort in derision. She turned toward him. "Eugene was a meticulous man. Also rather vain. He would no more have confronted Ronnie and dressed him down without his teeth in his mouth than he would go out on an interview that way. He might have been shirtless, but Ronnie was probably the only person who ever saw him in his underwear. Still, if Eugene had to face that snotty teenager, he wouldn't have done so toothless. Ronnie would have described him that way to every kid in town."

"Yeah, you're probably right," Torgeson agreed. "So he didn't expect Ronnie home before he went to bed."

"No."

"Well, I'll leave you guys to it," Walt said, pushing himself away from the doorjamb where he had been leaning and sauntering off toward the coffee pot.

"Okay," Clay returned to his theme. "Eugene got home at eight thirty. He had a nice fire going in the fireplace, so he took off his wool shirt and went around with only his underwear. Well, he still had his pants on. He was wearing socks and slippers. That, Erica thinks, means he wasn't expecting any company." He gave her a questioning glance and she nodded. "At ten, he made his regular phone call to Sarah, but instead of talking for ten minutes, he only talked for two or three because Sarah had to go put her car in the carport. So at some time between then and when it quit snowing, he took his teeth out, got his pills and a glass of water and went into the living room, where he set the pills and the water on the little table beside his easy chair. He'd probably just done that, because he hadn't taken the pills. He'd turned off the electric heater for the night, which meant that the fire was still going enough to be comfortable in the room without his shirt. Then, much to his surprise, someone came through the door, without knocking."

"Herb Schultz," Torgeson stated with a little too much emphasis, as if trying to convince himself.

"You're nuts!" Erica asserted.

The sheriff turned toward her and grinned. "I'll take your badge back if you don't show proper respect to your boss."

"You don't believe it yourself," Erica challenged.

"What makes you think that?"

"The way you act…"

"How should we act?"

"…and because Clay is working his butt off trying to figure out what happened." She gestured toward the piles of evidence.

"I have to be able to present a coherent case, even if we know who did it."

"But you're having trouble aren't you?"

Clay flushed.

"And besides, out there at the cabin on Sunday morning, Kline had already arrested Herb, but you two were looking for evidence, and when Clay said the slug was from either a thirty-thirty or a thirty-ought-six, Pete remarked that ninety percent of the homes around here had one or the other; to which you, Clay, said that meant you had lots of suspects. You two didn't suspect Herb at that time, and I don't think you do now."

Silence descended over the room. The clock on the wall ticked away the seconds. Muffled sounds from outside the room occasionally penetrated its interior. Finally, Torgeson shifted his bulk, rose to his feet and said to Clay. "I'll leave you to get on with it. Erica, he's got a lot of work to do. The preliminary hearing is Monday."

"Right! I'll get out of your hair." She turned toward Clay, who hadn't moved. "But don't let your desire to railroad Herb blind you to the obvious problems with your case against him."

*   *   *

Erica stalked out of the sheriff's office, down the stairs and out into the frigid air. Her Jeep was cold and hadn't time to warm up on the drive back to her clinic. She parked it in the garage and went through the house, shedding her coat, hat and gloves on her way down the stairs to the office.

There, sitting on a bench in the waiting room, still clad for the out-of-doors, sat Kelly. The girl rose as Erica entered, turned to face her employer and stated, "I've got a job with Dr. Somers, starting this morning. I want my paycheck."

CHAPTER 19

Erica stood and stared at Kelly, both her body and brain momentarily paralyzed. She had heard the words but her conscious mind refused to comprehend them. It couldn't happen! Not now! Therefore it didn't happen, her brain told her. She forced fingers of reality to penetrate the barricade her mind had erected.

"You can't."

"I can, and I'm going to right now. I want my paycheck."

"But we have the cystotomy to do this morning."

Kelly shrugged. "That's not my problem."

I'll jolly well make it your problem, thought Erica.

"You have a responsibility to give me adequate notice if you want to leave. I won't do anything to hinder you, but you owe me the courtesy to stay on until I can find a replacement to do the critical things that are on the schedule."

"I'm going and that's that."

"Kelly, please stay for a couple of hours to let me get this surgery done."

"Why don't you send it down to Trent to do. *He* could handle it."

"*I* can handle it, but it's not fair of you to leave me in the lurch like this."

Again Kelly shrugged.

"Kelly, think of the dog. Don't you care about her? You have an obligation to the patient, even if you don't feel you have any obligation to me."

"Trent said you'd be like that."

"Like what?"

"He said you'd try to get out of paying me."

That did it! Any state of denial Erica might have found herself in was suddenly gone; replaced by a state of cold, hard rage.

"I have *not* refused to pay you and you know it. You also know that you've always gotten your paycheck on time, that you've been paid appropriately for any overtime you did, and that I've never tried to hold anything back or cheat you in any way. If Dr. Somers said that, he is guilty of slander, and you should have set him straight."

Kelly shifted uneasily. "Just give me my check," she begged in a voice that lacked its former surly conviction.

"All right. I'll make out your check, but don't ever ask me for a reference. In fact, I'll tell everyone I know exactly what happened." Erica spun on her heel, marched to her office and snatched the checkbook off a shelf. She looked up Kelly's hours worked, figured the payroll deductions, and wrote out the check. Tearing it out of the book, she whirled and handed it to Kelly, who perched expectantly in the doorway. Kelly scanned the check and frowned.

"Don't I get a bonus?"

"*Bonus!* What the hell makes you think you deserve a bonus?"

"Well, you said you'd make it up to me for losing time this week."

Erica sighed and explained as one might to a small child, "I meant that in future weeks, when things picked up, I'd try to do something extra for you. You would have to be working here."

"I still think I should get a bonus."

"A bonus is not only a reward for past work, it is given as an incentive to encourage good performance in the future. You have a lot of nerve asking me for a bonus when you're leaving me without advance notice, when you know I have surgery scheduled and need you here. I should dock your check instead."

Kelly scrutinized the check to make certain that Erica had not actually done so. Her lower lip stuck out in a pout, she whined, "It's not fair!"

"What, exactly, is not fair?"

"Well…"

"Nothing. I've been fair with you. It's you who has not been fair with me. Now beat it. I've got work to do."

With dragging steps, Kelly walked to the door, turned as if to say something else, but seeing Erica turn her back, made her way out into the freezing morning.

"Good riddance," Erica muttered. She turned to her desk to complete the paperwork involved with her payroll. On the check stub, she deducted the amount of Kelly's check. Her bank balance now showed exactly $1.89.

*   *   *

"What the hell's going on over there with that asshole, Schultz?"

It was Jewel Kline's usual morning mood, but this time her husband was on the defensive. "Just give us time."

"You've already had a week? How long does it take you to get a confession out of an old idiot like that?"

"It's not a week. It's only five days."

"So five days; a week. What difference does it make?"

"The preliminary hearing is Monday. After that it should be smooth sailing."

"Are you sure?"

"Sure I'm sure."

"That's not what I hear around town. Ever since Vanderpool took the case, everyone's saying he'll get Schultz off."

"I've beat him once. That's why I'm in office and he's out."

"You didn't beat him in court."

Lyle Kline didn't have an answer to that.

*　*　*

Erica Merrill may have given the sheriff's office some interesting information, but it didn't solve the problem of how to present a convincing case at the upcoming preliminary hearing.

"Our case still has some holes in it, doesn't it?" Pete Torgeson asked, pulling out a chair opposite Clay and turning it around. He straddled the chair, leaning his arms on the back.

"Like a sieve," was his deputy's reply. "And when Otis Vanderpool gets done with us, it will be ventilated even more."

"You got any good ideas?"

Clay pushed his chair away from the table and leaned back, balancing it on two legs. "I've got one suggestion."

"Shoot."

"Let Walt Forgey question him. Kline doesn't know how to get anything out of a guy like Schultz. Herb gets his goat. He blows smoke in Kline's face and dares Kline to make him quit smoking. He knows he has Kline on the run. But Walt might know what buttons to push to get Herb talking. They grew up in the same environment. They speak the same language. If anyone can get anything out of him, Walt probably can."

"That sounds reasonable. Can't hurt anyway."

The sheriff heaved himself off the chair and lumbered out the door. Clay could hear him calling, "Hey, Walt. Come here a minute."

In the meantime, thought Clay, *I'd better get back to work on this stuff.* He settled down once again to go over the evidence.

* * *

Word filtered around the town that Herb Schultz continued to maintain his innocence. In pairs and in clusters, Boulder's inhabitants discussed who else might have killed Eugene Pettijohn. They talked in the taverns and in the coffee shop; on the streets and around the mail boxes; at work and in the halls of the courthouse. Lena Lemm summed up the opinion of the populace when, leaning across the fence which divided their properties, she said to Carl Nelson, "I bet them Dibble boys did it."

"Yeah," Carl replied. "They were up to something Saturday night, and you can bet your bottom dollar it was something fishy."

At the sheriff's office, Clay Caldwell said to himself, "Damn! I wish I could get hold of those Dibble kids."

Jackie Dibble heard the conversations, or noticed the sudden silences when her presence became known, and shivered.

* * *

Clara Merrill could not interest herself in whether or not Herb Schultz had killed Eugene Pettijohn. That was a matter for the experts to figure out. She had confidence in the sheriff, and in Clay, his deputy. She knew Otis Vanderpool to be a very competent lawyer. She doubted the capability of the new county attorney, Lyle Kline, but reasoned that the skill of the other men would outweigh his lack. She thought of all experts as men.

She realized that her granddaughter, Erica, was trying to crack the dominance of the male hierarchy, but being from another generation, one which bowed to the will of men, she questioned whether this was appropriate.

She wanted to help. She could see that Erica was under a great deal of stress, that her practice was not doing well, and that her finances were in poor shape. Clara Merrill had one sure-fire remedy for all this anxiety. Erica should seek the help and advice of her father, Hugh.

*　　*　　*

At noon, Walt Forgey, who had been talking to Herb Schultz in the latter's cell, let himself out of the jail, found Pete Torgeson and shook his head.

"We went over his whole police record and a whole lot of other stuff. I was trying to find a lever, so I could pry something loose from him. But he doesn't care. He knows that we know his entire past, so he doesn't mind talking about it. Admits he used to get in a lot of fights."

"He does have a record of violence."

"Yeah, but look at it. He gets in barroom brawls. He fights with his fists; at least he used to. He's not much for fighting any more. Getting too old. Sure he busted a few jaws and cracked a few ribs on guys that tried to fight him, but he never used any weapon. The only time there was a weapon involved, some guy pulled a knife on him and he took it away. He didn't use it, just took it away from this other guy."

"Yeah, but now that he's older, he may feel he needs an advantage. He and Pettijohn never did get along."

"No, they didn't. But that's another thing. Herb never was one for holding a grudge. He could fight a guy one night and belly up to the bar with him the next."

"Christ! I hate this case," the sheriff exclaimed.

"Look here," Walt Forgey dropped his voice. "About those tracks. Are you sure Clay knows what he's talking about?"

*   *   *

Erica's emotions were in turmoil. She needed an assistant in order to do the surgery. She racked her brain but could not come up with a single name of a person who might be able to help. She even thought of calling her sister-in-law, Heather, but the last time Heather had watched a surgery, she had fainted. Erica didn't need another patient on her hands while she was in the midst of an operation.

Could she do it alone? She knew that some vets did, but she was not comfortable with the thought. Nevertheless, she went over in her mind what she would have to do.

It would require getting the surgery room completely ready before anesthetizing the dog. Even opening the packs. Erica was uncomfortable with that; it meant possible contamination. Perhaps she could leave the packs until the dog was on the table. That would require longer anesthesia, and would distract her attention from the patient in the critical early stages of anesthesia.

There lay the main problem. She would have to divide her attention between the state of the patient and the technical matters related to the surgery itself. She could get wrapped up in the surgical procedure and not notice a deteriorating condition until too late. Or she might have to deal with an anesthetic emergency, leaving the surgical site open, draining urine into the abdomen, becoming contaminated.

The dog was healthy and a good surgical candidate (what a funny phrase), so nothing was likely to go wrong, she reasoned. Yet, this was a valuable dog, one she liked very well, and owned by a client who had bucked the recent trend and brought the dog to her, trusting her competence and judgment.

Still, other vets did this sort of thing all the time.

What were her alternatives?

She could send the dog down to Trent, or even take it to one of the vets in Lincoln. To do so would imply failure, lack of ability to do a simple surgery. Word would get around. She would lose more clients and be the laughing stock of the local vets.

Still, if she attempted the surgery and the dog died, things would be much worse. She could even be accused of malpractice.

Pride warred with caution and pride won. She would do the surgery, all by herself.

CHAPTER 20

Erica brought the dog, Belle, in from the run where she had left her early that morning. Belle couldn't figure out why she wasn't getting any breakfast. What she got instead was an assortment of pre-anesthetic injections. She gave Erica a forlorn look, as if saying, *What did I do to deserve such treatment?*

While the injections took effect, Erica got out the sterile surgery packs: instruments, surgical gown, gloves, scrub brush, drapes, extra towels, a pan to put the stones in when they were removed from the bladder. She puzzled over how to manage a syringe of sterile saline solution to flush out the bladder, and possibly more to flush the abdominal cavity if any urine drained into it, though she hoped to avoid the latter problem.

She turned on the telephone answering machine so she wouldn't have to worry about the phone, readied the anesthesia machine, and was about to take the dog out of her cage, when the outer door opened, bringing in a blast of cold air. Erica went to the waiting room to see who had come.

There, in parka and boots, her curly auburn hair poking out from under the hood, stood Erica's childhood chum, Lauren Dunbar, a surgical nurse at the Lincoln Hospital.

"There is a God!" Erica crowed with delight.

"Really?" Lauren's laughing face seemed a bit startled at this greeting.

They hugged each other. Erica pushed Lauren back to arm's length, surveyed her from head to toe, and chortled, "Lauren, you're looking great. Are you on vacation, or are you just buzzing through?"

"I have a few days off. I'll tell you all about it later. How are things going with you? And what's this 'There is a God' stuff?"

"Lauren, I've had a crisis. I have surgery that has to be done today and my assistant quit this morning. I'll tell *you* more about *that* later, but tell me, could you help me with my surgery?"

"Sure. If I can. What do you want me to do?"

"I need someone to monitor the anesthesia and to open packs and help me into my gown. I can actually get into it by myself, but trying to juggle everything and keep an eye on the patient at the same time seems rather daunting. I'd also need you to help me flush things with sterile saline. I'd tell you exactly what I wanted done. Being a surgical nurse, you'll probably consider it rather primitive."

"I've watched quite a few veterinary surgeries, on everything from cats to bulls. I'm actually a nurse in the recovery room, so monitoring vital signs is right up my alley. You'll have to show me what to watch for with dogs, though."

"Oh, Lauren! You're a life-saver!"

Lauren shed her outdoor garments and Erica gave her a scrub top and set out an extra cap and mask, while describing what she would need Lauren to do. She pointed out the various surgery packs and supplies, gave her a quick course on operating the anesthesia machine and showed her where the emergency drugs were kept.

"I'll tell you the anesthetic and oxygen flow levels as we go, and if we need any emergency drugs, I'll tell you the dose."

For Lauren, this was all easy, her training in human surgical assisting only needing to be adapted to canine requirements. "Okay. I think I can handle all that," she remarked calmly.

"Now, the first thing you need to do is the hardest. Hold the dog while I mask her down."

Lauren laughed. "No problem. I've held farm dogs while Dad pulled porcupine quills out of them."

Erica placed the anesthetic mask over the dog's muzzle and turned on the gases. After a brief struggle, the dog went limp, and Lauren took over as anesthetist while Erica scrubbed. Lauren then divided her attention between being anesthetist and surgical nurse during the operation. Everything went off without a hitch.

The surgery was "uneventful," a euphemism which means that no disaster struck. When Erica opened the bladder and started removing stones, Lauren gasped in amazement. "How long did it take her to produce all those stones?"

"A year or so, I'd guess."

"Good grief! Why didn't they get her taken care of earlier?"

"They didn't notice. She's a working ranch dog, out of doors all the time. Her owner finally saw blood in the snow."

The surgery finished, they turned off the anesthetic gas but left her breathing oxygen. Belle was awake within a few minutes of being put back in her cage.

The surgeon and her nurse slapped hands in a high-five.

*   *   *

When they were sure their patient was out of danger, as evidenced by her waking up and wagging her stub of a tail whenever they opened the cage, the two friends went upstairs for a cup of coffee. Clara Merrill, who had always treated Lauren like another granddaughter, was delighted to see her. The three settled down around the fireplace in the living room for a good time of catching up on each other's lives. The Siamese cat abandoned Gram and made a beeline for Lauren, sniffing her up one side and down the other.

"She's reading the paper," Gram remarked, and Lauren howled with laughter. Apparently liking the news she read with her nose, Orphan Annie leapt gracefully into Lauren's lap and settled down, purring contentedly.

"Where'd you get this neat cat?"

"She belonged to Eugene Pettijohn. She was in the only warm room of the house, hiding under the bed, when Eugene was found on Sunday morning," Erica explained.

"So you're boarding her."

"Actually, she has now been officially given to Gram. None of Eugene's heirs wants her. At least none but Ronnie. He hasn't been asked, but it's kind of up in the air where he will be living."

"Hmm. That's a problem, isn't it? I wonder what they'll do with him?"

"I don't know. Right now he's living with the couple who run the jail."

Lauren made a face. "How jolly."

"I have a new 'assistant' and I'll bet you'll never guess who," Erica smirked.

"In that case, I won't try."

"Would you believe, the youngest Dibble boy?"

"What?"

"I told you you'd never guess."

"You were right about that!"

"Actually, he's not like the others. He is nine years old, bright, cheerful, loves school, thinks his teacher is great, and has promised to tell his older brothers that there's no use breaking into my clinic looking for money or drugs because there isn't enough to be worth stealing."

"Now that last part sounds more like the Dibbles."

"He has been hired as official cat petter and dog walker and he gets paid in cookies."

Lauren shook her head. "Erey, I'll never figure you out. You never impressed me as one who would be taking an interest in children."

"Guess who got me started on that."

"I'm past guessing."

"Mr. McMurtry. We were talking about the Dibbles and he remarked that if Mrs. McMurtry were still alive, she would probably try to find a way to get that child out of the Dibble household. He and I both think the boy, Eddie Lee, is not Jess Dibble's son."

Erica heard Gram gasp, but such news did not shock Lauren. She gazed out the window thinking, then said, "I wonder who his father is then. In fact, I could make a guess on that one."

"Oh!"

"Ten years ago, Jackie Dibble helped nurse Dick Thom's brother who was recuperating from surgery for cancer, pancreatic if I remember correctly. I don't recall the brother's name."

"If he was the boy's father, they certainly kept it secret."

"And we should do likewise," Lauren emphasized firmly.

Erica nodded. "Right! We should."

They sat in silence for a few moments, enjoying being together. Erica broke the silence.

"Speaking of Mr. McMurtry, he invited me for tea this afternoon at two. Why don't you come, Lauren? He would be delighted to see you."

"I can't. I promised to be back home for lunch. I should leave before long. But I get the impression you're strapped for help. Maybe I could fill in until you get someone."

"Do you have that much time off?"

"I filled in for other nurses over the holidays, so I have five days in a row off, starting today. And you have probably heard that we may go on strike."

Erica groaned. "Yes, I did. I'm not sure I approve of medical personnel striking. It seems to me that everything in the health care system is behind, and I can't see that striking would do anything else but get things farther behind. What do you gain?"

"Money. Time off. Things like that. But I'm not sure it's worth it. I'm like you. I have a gut dislike of striking, but I will say that we do have arguments on our side. Still, I'd rather not. I'm up for promotion in the near future. I'll be supervising the recovery ward, if I get the promotion."

"Really! That's great! You've come a long way in a few ycars. I wouldn't have thought someone so young would be given a position like that, but I'm sure you can handle it."

"I was surprised myself. It's a real challenge. If I have to go on strike it might not come about. So I went to our head nurse and laid everything on the line. We decided that I should take these five days, then if there is a strike, take my accumulated vacation time, which is a little over two weeks. That way, I won't officially be a striker. Then if we're still on strike, I'll have to go out, but the head nurse says she doesn't think that will be held against me."

"So that gives you about three weeks all together."

"Right."

"Well, I can't offer you anything to match being supervisor of the recovery ward, and I certainly can't pay you anywhere near as much, but if you could help me out from time to time, I'd appreciate it."

"You don't have to pay me."

"Lauren! Don't be silly."

"No, really. I had a ball this morning."

"I wouldn't think you would be interested in veterinary surgery after the stuff you've done."

"But I am. Do you know what I like best about it?"

"What?"

"The personal relationship with the patient. That's why I like recovery ward work, too. You are dealing with people, not machines. Actual surgical assisting started to get me down. I did that over in Seattle at the University hospital. They do such fancy stuff there, you get the impression that the focus is on the equipment and not on the patient. Sometimes you lose track of the fact that there is a real blood and guts person under all the drapes and machines. This morning, it was always obvious that the patient was there, and that you never lost your main focus, which was to help that patient."

"Thanks, Lauren."

"Besides, Erica, you're a damn good surgeon."

"Ha! Go tell that to Trent Somers!"

*　　*　　*

Erica decided to walk to the McMurtry house, but after scrambling up the hillside for three blocks on ice-covered sidewalks, she questioned her decision. By the time she got there, her nose, the only appendage not covered by wool or fleece, was nearly frozen and she was out of breath. Her eyes ached from the glare of sunlight on the glittering snow.

Mr. McMurtry welcomed her into his basement suite, which opened directly onto the lawn at the rear of the house and had a view over the valley and the town.

"You look frozen. I have just the thing for you," he said. As Erica divested herself of parka, scarf, cap and boots, he disappeared into his small kitchenette, returning shortly with two steaming mugs.

"Mulled wine," he said.

"Wonderful! I can certainly use it."

She wrapped her hands around the mug and held her nose over its steaming top, letting both the warmth and the aroma do their work.

"I thought it might go over even better than tea on a day like this."

"Mr. McMurtry, you're a genius."

They sipped their wine in contented silence for several minutes, then the old teacher spoke.

"How is it going? The practice, I mean."

"I don't know. I've hardly had anything to do this week."

"The cold weather, no doubt."

"I hope that's all it is. I'm nearly broke."

"And you want to make it on your own, not lean on your dad."

"Exactly."

"You will. Everyone has problems at the start of a new business venture. You will succeed. Just wait and see."

"I'm glad you have faith in me."

They talked for a while about McMurtry's retirement plans. The conversation eventually drifted back to the days when he was teaching, and inevitably ended up in a comparison of students old and new.

"One thing hasn't changed," the teacher remarked. "I have never been able to make much impact on the grammar of the local kids. They don't hear good grammar at home, so what they learn in school is never put to use. I've had two generations, and the start of a third, of children who never will learn how to speak or write correctly because their parents, some of them ones I have tried to teach, don't use good grammar."

"It must be frustrating."

"Take pronouns, for example. A pronoun should have an antecedent, a noun which names the person or object being referred to. This antecedent should be obvious, and the same pronoun should not be used for more than one in the same sentence. I became frustrated trying to read the students' stories or essays where I couldn't tell who or what was being referred to. It's not so bad in speech, because you can stop the speaker and ask if you become confused. But in writing…"

McMurtry continued on with his dissertation, but Erica had stopped listening. She sat frozen, the mug half-way to her lips. The teacher finally noticed and paused to regard her quizzically.

"Where gottest thou that goose look?"

"Well you might ask. Goose look is right," she responded, for she had recalled a conversation exactly like that, a very significant conversation. "May I use your phone?"

"Certainly. Do you need a directory?"

"Yes, please."

"It's in the drawer under the phone."

Erica flipped the pages and found the number she wanted. She dialed, and the phone rang and rang. There was no answer.

CHAPTER 21

While she was slipping and sliding back down the hillside to her clinic, Erica noted that the waning daylight was darker than it had been for the last week. Instead of the clear, bright cold, the atmosphere had a dim, hazy appearance. She looked down the valley and saw thick clouds massing over the western horizon. She groaned. I hope we're not in for another snowstorm, she thought.

She tried the phone number again, letting it ring a dozen times before she hung up. She checked her surgery patient, who wanted out. Erica put the dog in the outside run. How *any* animal could want out in this bitter cold was beyond her comprehension. She called the number again, with the same result.

Erica knew that her anxiety to reach the person she was trying to call was unreasonable. That person would be back eventually. Nothing critical hung in the balance, needing urgently to be resolved. Yet once the thought had occurred to her, Erica's desire to verify it overwhelmed her. She paced the floor, eyeing the phone and forcing herself to wait at least fifteen minutes before she called again. When she did, the phone rang hollowly in an empty house.

She could hardly eat supper. She had not been eating well of late, and Gram had become concerned. Gram attempted to stimulate her granddaughter's appetite with Erica's favorite foods, but Erica hardly seemed to notice. Gram wished that the murder case would be resolved soon, and that life would return to some semblance of normal. She could not understand why Erica wanted to become involved.

Erica pushed her plate away and got up. "I have to make a call." Again the phone rang and rang and no one answered.

"You seem really nervous tonight," Gram remarked.

"I have an important call to make and I can't get through."

"It can't be *that* important."

"No. You're right. But it frustrates me that I can't get hold of anyone and find out whether I'm right or not."

"About your surgery case?"

"No. But that reminds me. I ought to call that rancher and tell him Belle's doing all right. I couldn't get him either when I tried earlier."

Erica brought the dog in from the outside run and put her back in her cage. Belle circled around two or three times, then dropped to the cage floor with a thump, not on the blanket, but on the bare metal.

"You silly dog," Erica remarked affectionately. Belle wagged her stub of a tail. Erica gave her half a bowl of water. "If you keep that down, you can have some food." The dog lapped up every drop and looked up at Erica expectantly. She waited to see that the dog kept the water down, then gave her a small bowl of canned dog food. It disappeared in two gulps. Again, Belle eyed Erica anxiously, awaiting the next installment. "A little bit at a time. Be patient."

She should take her own advice, she scolded herself. She had tried the phone number several more times.

In the meantime, she called the rancher. This time, he answered his phone.

"Belle's doing fine. She is up and around, wants out in the cold, and has eaten and drunk a small amount."

"That's great, Doc. When can I come get her?"

"If the weather stays clear, you could take her home tomorrow, but it looks as if we might have another storm. I think it would be best if you left her here. It's not likely that anything would go wrong, but in case it did, you wouldn't want to be stuck way out there with no way to bring her in."

"Yeah, I guess you're right. Give me a call when you think it's all right to pick her up. And thanks, Doc."

Erica dialed the other number again. She listened idly as it rang two times, then was startled as there was a click on the line, followed by a woman's voice saying, "Hello."

"Hello, Sarah. This is Erica Merrill. I'm glad I got you. I've been trying since mid-afternoon."

Sarah laughed. "The kids took me out for a drive, to see what the land looks like with all this snow, since the roads are pretty good now. Then we went to the Whitewater Steakhouse down the river for supper. They're going home to Tacoma tomorrow."

"I hope the weather stays good for them. Listen. I'd like to ask you a question. I hope you don't mind."

"Oh, I don't mind." Sarah was obviously in an expansive mood. "What do you want to know?"

"It's about the gun. Did Eugene call you and tell you Ronnie could have it back, or did he tell you in person?"

"It wasn't Eugene who told me. It was Ronnie."

"You mean, Ronnie came to your place and told you that Eugene said he could have the gun?"

"That's right."

"And you believed him?"

"Sure. He didn't know that he'd left it at my house, so he must have told him."

"You mean that, because Ronnie knew that you had the gun, you figured that Eugene had to have told him."

"That's right."

How stupid could this woman get? Erica asked herself in exasperation. Ronnie would have guessed right off the bat that the place Eugene would have taken the gun was Sarah's house. A kid like that could wrap a woman like Sarah around his little finger.

"You didn't check it out with Eugene?"

"I didn't have to. Ronnie was real nice and pleasant…"

I'll bet! Erica thought uncharitably.

"…and he explained everything and said he was real sorry he'd acted the way he did, but he knew that was wrong and was going to behave himself and handle the gun the way he was supposed to. He said he was going to give him more lessons."

"Eugene was?"

"Yes."

"So you got the gun and gave it to him?"

"Oh, no! I wouldn't handle one of those things! When he brought it over, he put it in the closet, and when he came to get it, I told him where to find it and he went and got it."

"So you didn't handle it at all."

"Not me!"

"Thanks Sarah. Oh, by the way, is it snowing out at your place?"

"I don't know. Let me look."

There was a pause, then Sarah came back on the line. "You're right! It's snowing like crazy."

"I hope your car is in the carport."

"Yes, it is, thank God."

"But I think Jennie and Dan are going to have to stay over another day or two."

*   *   *

As soon as she broke the connection with Sarah, Erica hastily dialed another number. To her immense relief, Clay picked it up on the first ring.

"Hi Erica." He sounded glad to hear from her.

"Clay, can you come over? I've got something to tell you."

Clay groaned. "Not again!"

"This is important."

"Can't you tell me on the phone?"

"It would be much better if you come over here. Clay, I can tell you who killed Eugene and how it was done."

There was silence on the line.

"Clay, I'm serious."

"This had better be good."

"Will you please give me credit for once for knowing what I'm talking about? I'll tell you where you can get the evidence to show how Eugene was killed."

"I don't suppose you'll give me any peace unless I come over there, so I'll come."

"Thanks Clay. Come to the clinic door. I'll see you in a few minutes."

It was only five minutes before Clay's pickup turned into the parking lot. Erica opened the door for him, and he came in, stamping snow off his boots.

"Hey, did you know it's started to snow again?"

"I can see that. That's all we need."

Clay shed his coat and hung it on the coat rack. "Now, what's this big news you have to tell me?"

"Sit down."

Clay did as he was bidden, plopping down on a bench in the waiting room. Erica sat opposite him, leaning forward, her forearms resting on her knees.

"Let me go back to last Sunday. Remember when Sarah Pettijohn came over to the cabin and you questioned her about Eugene's rifle?"

"Yes. Sure."

"Do you remember what she told you?"

"She said that Eugene had given her the rifle to hide away from Ronnie, because he didn't think Ronnie was responsible enough to handle it."

"And…?"

"That he told her that Ronnie could have it back again. So Ronnie went and got it."

"*Who* told her that Ronnie could have it back?"

"Why, Eugene did!"

Erica shook her head. "You're wrong. That's what I thought also, until I was visiting Mr. McMurtry this afternoon and he was complaining about the difficulty he had trying to teach grammar to the local kids. He gave as a specific example, the misuse of pronouns."

Clay sat there frowning, wondering what this had to do with the murder.

Erica continued, "He said that many people don't understand that a pronoun needs to refer to a person or thing that is also named, usually in the same sentence, and that one pronoun should not be used for more than one person or thing. That sentence of Sarah's popped into my mind. We all assumed that it was Eugene who told Sarah that Ronnie could have the gun back, because that seemed most logical to us. But that's not what happened. I called Sarah. Instead of telling her she had her grammar all wrong, and getting her back up, I asked her whether Eugene had told her over the phone or in person that Ronnie could come and get the gun."

"But that's ridiculous! She wouldn't have given it to him on that basis."

"You or I wouldn't, without checking with Eugene, if we had been in that situation. But Sarah did. When I asked her why she didn't check with Eugene, she said she didn't have to because Ronnie didn't know where Eugene had hidden the gun, so she figured that since he *did* know, Eugene must have told him."

"Good grief! I don't believe it. No one could be that dumb."

"But she was. Ronnie went down there and soft-soaped her and walked away with the rifle."

Clay shook his head in disbelief.

"Clay, were there any fingerprints on that gun?"

"Yes. A lot of them were wiped off when the gun was cleaned, but there were several of Eugene's, and quite a few of Ronnie's. But they would naturally have been on it. There weren't any of Herb's if you're wondering about that."

"None of Sarah's?"

"No."

"Good. She said she hadn't actually handled the gun herself. That's another thing we got wrong, though I doubt that it matters. Just now, you said that Eugene gave the gun to Sarah to hide, but actually, Sarah was afraid to touch it. She had Eugene put it in a closet, and when Ronnie came to get it, she had him go to the closet himself. It goes to show that we can read things into what other people say that aren't really there. At least we know, from Eugene's character, that the gun was unloaded."

"Okay, so Ronnie got the gun under false pretenses. That doesn't surprise me. I can't see that it makes any difference. Not until Eugene found out about it. Then he'd have had the kid's hide."

"But it changes the scenario that you sketched out."

"How?"

"Don't you see? If Ronnie had gone to the house while Eugene was out, done a sloppy cleaning job, and put the gun on the rack, Eugene would have noticed it immediately when he got home."

"Yeah, he would have."

"The fact that he was getting ready for bed, that he'd made his usual call to Sarah, *without saying anything about the gun,* and that he wasn't expecting to meet or talk to anyone that night, means that his rifle was not on the rack over the fireplace when Eugene was shot."

Clay nodded. "Go on."

"Here's what I think happened. Ronnie got hold of the rifle, by dishonest means, taking advantage of his aunt's gullibility. He showed it off to the other boys, and since one had a shell, which we can assume was a thirty-thirty, they loaded the gun and went out to the rifle range. It was closed, so they decided to put off shooting the gun until the next day, when Ronnie probably thought he could sneak some of Eugene's shells out of the box and they could all have a go at it.

"So they hung around town, or at someone's house for most of the evening. Remember, it wasn't cold yet, so they could have been outside all the time. Someone may have seen them. Anyway, along toward ten, Ronnie left the other kids and went out to the cabin. I think he probably planned to sneak the gun into the house while Eugene was on the phone. He knew Eugene's routine—that he would call Sarah at ten and talk for at least ten minutes. So I suspect that Ronnie thought he could get the gun into the house and hidden in his room while Eugene was on the phone. He would aim for about five after ten.

"The phone is in the kitchen, and you can't see into the living room from there. Ronnie's bedroom opened off the living room. But Eugene could have seen Ronnie drive his car into the driveway from where he was in the kitchen, so I think Ronnie probably parked out on the road. He may have been going to nip in and out again and then drive up, pretending that he had just gotten home, or he may have planned to go out again."

"But Erica…"

"Wait a minute. Hear me out. I don't know whether Eugene would have left the door unlocked, or whether Ronnie had a key. Do you know?"

"He would have left it unlocked if he expected Ronnie back, even though the boy had a key. Ronnie told us that. That's why we knew Herb could have gotten in."

"Well, things didn't go according to plan. Ronnie opened the door, stepped into the room, and there was Eugene standing by the fireplace, staring at him. They were probably both equally surprised. Why he did it, I don't know, but I think Ronnie must have swung the gun up and fired a shot before Eugene had a chance to react. It was point-blank range, and Ronnie is reputed to be a good shot, thanks to Eugene's tutoring."

"I can't see him stopping to clean the gun," Clay objected.

"He may have done it out of sheer reflex, or he may have done it deliberately. Ronnie isn't dumb. He would know that a dirty gun on the rack would be a dead giveaway that it was the murder weapon, because Eugene was so meticulous. So he did a really quick job of cleaning it, threw it up on the rack and beat it so fast he didn't even close the door or the gate."

"But Erica, it couldn't have happened that way. The tracks!"

"Oh, you and your damn tracks," she said with irritation. "There weren't any tracks…"

"But. . ."

"…because their wasn't any snow!"

"Now you have gone completely bonkers," Clay shouted.

"Calm down and let me finish."

Clay held his head in his hands and sighed loudly.

"George McLeod, Trent Somers and I went to a conference in Lincoln Saturday night, in Trent's car. It was just ten o'clock when we let George out at his place down on the river and a few flakes of snow were falling.

"Sarah Pettijohn lives about a quarter of a mile up the creek from George's place. She noticed it snowing hard at about two or three minutes after ten. Trent let me out in front of this house and I was still standing out by the street when the first gust of wind hit and the snow started coming down. I went in the house and Gram heard me come in. She scolded me for being late. I was due back at ten. So I looked at my watch. It was ten after. It must have started snowing about eight minutes after ten.

"Clay, weather systems move west to east. That one was coming up the valley from the west. Now the ridge is east of town and I'd guess that Eugene's cabin is about as far east of this house as we are from George's. It took eight minutes for the storm to get from the river up here. It would take about the same time for it to move on up to the ridge. Say ten fifteen, just to round things off.

"Ronnie had a good ten minutes to shoot Eugene, clean the gun and beat it out of the house before the snow hit."

Clay sat there staring at Erica in silence, trying to take it in.

Erica went on, "Just to show you I'm not talking through my hat, when I called Sarah tonight, the last thing I asked her was whether it was snowing down there. She looked out the window and said it was snowing like crazy. You got here less than ten minutes after that and you said, 'It's *starting* to snow.'"

She let that sink in, then said, "Then Ronnie hurried down to Mabel's and probably made a nuisance of himself to impress upon the people there that he'd been waiting for Lolita for a while. He must have told her he had money, because she left with him. You know the rest of *that* story."

"I suppose it could have happened like that."

"I said I'd tell you how you can prove it."

"How?"

"Your old coach, Mr. Kinch, taught us all about weather. Remember?"

Clay nodded.

"For years, he has been the local observer for the weather bureau. I'll bet that if you went over there and asked him, he could tell you exactly when it started snowing at his house, which is at the base of the ridge, about half way between here and the cabin. Mr. Kinch is a perfectionist, like Eugene. I'll bet he'll know."

Clay hesitantly got to his feet. "I'll go ask Coach. If you're right, I'll have to go tell Pete how you worked it out and let him take it from there."

"Oh no you don't!"

"What do you mean?"

"Clay, *you* are going to go out and solve this case. This will be your big break. You don't need to say anything about me. I'll get my kick out of seeing Kline with mud on his face. This is *your* case. You go clean it up."

Clay shrugged into his coat and moved irresolutely toward the door. "Erica, you'd better be right about this."

CHAPTER 22

By Saturday morning, the weather had changed dramatically. Wet snow drifted languidly down. Car tires swished through slush. The temperature hovered just under the freezing level. In spite of the snow, the residents of Boulder felt relief as the icy grip that the weather had held on the area was loosened.

Erica waited impatiently to hear from Clay. It was after ten before he phoned.

"Erica, you were right all along the line."

"Good! Tell me about it."

"I went over to Coach's house, like you suggested. You were right about the way he keeps records. He had to tell me everything there was to know about the weather last Saturday night. I only wanted the time the snow started, but I had to listen to all the rest of it before I found out. He said he knew a front was coming, so he kept a close eye on things that night. The snow started falling at his place at eleven minutes after ten. So you were dead on."

"Great! I'm glad it worked out that way. So then what happened?"

"I went over to Pete's house and laid it all out for him. He wasn't happy that the boy seemed to have done it, but he agreed that it probably happened the way you doped it out. He decided to wait until this morning to talk to Ronnie, and to do it at Jerry's house. That kid is having a rough time, since it hit him what he'd done. We thought it might be best to have Jerry's wife present. She's a mothering type and he might need her. Turns out he did.

"I think Ronnie sensed when we came to the house that we knew. He tried to bluff us, but Pete asked me to relate the whole sequence of events, without asking Ronnie any questions. At first, he was defiant, but as the story unfolded, you could see the astonishment on his face and watch his eyes widen. When I finished, he asked rather faintly, 'How did you know all that?'

"Then he sort of collapsed in a heap and Jerry's wife hugged him to her and comforted him. He cried for about five minutes. We just waited. Then we packed up his things and took him in. We put a suicide watch on him."

"So is Herb free now?"

"Yeah. We didn't think he'd mind spending another night in jail. And you know what? Pete's a real decent guy. He had me go out ahead of time to build a fire out at Herb's shack and warm the place up. Then he ordered some heating oil, paid for it himself, and told them to deliver it right away. He also had me go with Herb to the store and buy some groceries."

"That's really thoughtful of him."

"Herb will probably spend the evening in the Deerhorn, bragging about his experience, but Carl Nelson said he'd keep an eye on Herb and not let him get too drunk."

"He won't be the hero with that ex-deputy you were telling me about and his group of pals though."

"No, he won't. Those guys give me the creeps. Anyway, I put a bug in Herb's ear about you. I told him he owed his freedom to your efforts, and suggested a way he could show his appreciation."

"How?"

"Wait and see. Let's see if he really does it."

"Okay, keep me in suspense. How did Kline take all this?"

"Ha! He isn't even around. He got home last night and found a note from his wife. She and Mrs. Considine left their husbands identical notes saying they didn't want to live in this hick town any more, so they were flying to Las Vegas."

"*What!* "

"I guess they both cleaned out their joint bank accounts and left yesterday afternoon for Lincoln to catch their plane."

"Lyle Kline's no loss, but I hope we don't lose our doctor."

"I don't know about him, but Kline left first thing this morning to catch a flight to Vegas and the Lincoln County sheriff called us and said Kline had skidded into a ditch and missed his plane. Thought we might enjoy knowing. You could hear Pete laughing all over the building."

So that was it! That morning, Lauren had arrived with an account of meeting Dr. Considine at Boulder's little hospital where she had dropped in to visit the nurses. The doctor, whose demeanor was more commonly morose and dejected, had been practically skipping down the corridor, snapping his fingers and whistling a cheery tune.

Well, well!

* * *

On Wednesday, Herb Schultz showed up at Erica's clinic. For once he was clean-shaven, and he was wearing new clothes. He pulled a wad of bills from his pocket and said, "I come to pay my bill."

As Erica figured the total and wrote a receipt, Herb explained, "My sister Edna come over from Cottonwood yestidy. Her old man has money, so they said they'd pay old Otis for bein' my lawyer. When I got outta the clink, I was flat broke. They went and got me some new duds and give me some money to tide me over. That there depitty fella said

I owed you sumpin, and that I oughtta pay yore bill and git my dog fixed. When can you do that?"

"She'll have to wean her pups first. Do you have them back at your place?"

"Yeah, now it's warmed up, I went and got them. They're fine."

Erica eyed the money Herb held in his hand and suggested, "You might pay for the spay right now, then when she's ready, you can bring her in."

"Shore. That sounds good. How much?"

Erica quoted her fee and relieved Herb of some more of his roll of bills. He smiled at her. "Anyway, thanks a lot," he said, embarrassment showing in his voice.

Erica held out her hand and Herb engulfed it in his big paw. "You're welcome," she said.

Lauren Dunbar bounded in through the door immediately after Herb left.

"Was that Herb Schultz? I hardly recognized him."

"It was, and would you believe, he paid his bill."

*　　*　　*

There were other surprises during the week. As the residents of Boulder dug themselves out, life returned to normal. The practice picked up. One day, a lady called, saying that she was a neighbor of the owner of the little Poodle whose teeth Erica had pulled.

"She told me what a great job you did on that dog when the other vet wouldn't touch him. She was really pleased. My mutt needs his shots, so I thought I'd come to you."

One day, when Erica dropped into the AgriMaster store, which had changed a great deal from the days when it was run by Wilbur Pettijohn, but still was the best place in town to buy animal foods, she saw Belle's owner on the other side of the store. He spotted her, waved and yelled across the heads of the assembled customers, "Hey, Doc. Belle's doing great. No more blood. Thanks a lot."

A little advertising never hurts, thought Erica.

*　　*　　*

It was the following Sunday when everyone gathered in Gram's big living room to hear Clay tell them about the case. There were three generations of Merrills, two of Caldwells, as well as Lauren Dunbar and the two teachers, Alex McMurtry and Stew Kinch. They munched brownies and sipped coffee while Clay told the story. Then they began to speculate on the future.

"Does Ronnie have a lawyer?" Heather Merrill asked.

"Yeah. One of the lawyers from the firm in Lincoln that drew up Eugene's will is representing him. He's trying to plea bargain for a manslaughter charge instead of second degree murder."

"I thought Kline was opposed to plea bargaining," Erica remarked.

Clay grinned. "If he goes to court on this case, he'll be laughed right out of the county."

"Hey, that might be a good idea."

"Besides, that lawyer is a good friend of Otis Vanderpool, so they would sure make life miserable for Kline."

Those remarks brought on a round of merriment, as none of the assembled group had any love for the young county attorney.

"Then he'll be tried as an adult?" Heather looked concerned.

"Because of the seriousness of the charge, he'll be elevated to adult court. But I think his obvious remorse will be in his favor when it comes to sentencing. That kid is going through hell. It didn't hit him until they took him out to the cabin to get some clothes, the day after the murder was discovered, just what he'd done. Since then, he's been one sick boy. I heard that he could hardly make it through the funeral."

Alex McMurtry entered the conversation. "But why on earth did he shoot Eugene?"

Clay explained, "It seems that he really resented the rules Eugene laid down for him. He'd had no discipline in his own home, but Eugene was a lot more strict, and really laid down the law. I guess Ronnie was angry at having the rifle taken away from him, and when he went back to the house, trying to sneak it into his room, and Eugene caught him at it, he just lost his head and shot without thinking."

McMurtry shook his head and said sadly, "I don't know which is worse, too much discipline or too little."

"Anyway, too much coming after too little was a recipe for disaster," Erica observed.

"Everyone in his immediate family is now dead," Gram mused.

"Yes, but before you get too wrapped up in sympathy for him, remember it's his own fault," Hugh Merrill stated firmly.

"What happens to this money you say he has?" Clay's father asked.

"He won't inherit from Eugene, but he still has that trust fund. The bank agreed to let some of it be used for his legal expenses. They'll tie the rest of it up in the trust until sometime after he's out of prison. That will give him some money to get a start in life. You know, with most kids who get in serious trouble and go to prison early in life, they don't have anything when they come out and they quite easily fall back into a life of crime.

"Ronnie will have money for living expenses and an education. The trustees will dole it out. He won't have unlimited access to it, so they'll make sure it's used for something constructive."

"Still, it will be hard for him to get a start." Darrel Caldwell mused.

"It always is."

"Then who will get what Ronnie would otherwise have inherited?" Heather wanted to know.

"All the lawyers have put their heads together and got all the parties to agree to divvying it up in the same proportion as the rest of the inheritance. That is, Sarah and the charities Eugene named will each get one part. I don't mean that each charity will, but all of them together. The niece will get four parts. That's what they'll present to the probate court, which will probably go along with it."

"That makes sense," Darrel remarked.

"By the way, we found out what the Dibble kids were up to." Satisfaction showed on Clay's face.

"What were they doing?" Erica asked.

"They took one of their dogs to a dog fight. Not one of the hounds, a Pit Bull. Erica, I think you suspected that they kept fighting dogs."

"Yes, I did."

"We got an anonymous tip, complete with half a dozen names. We and three other sheriff's offices, one here in Idaho and two in Washington, held simultaneous raids in the wee small hours of this morning. The Dibbles had three dogs remaining. They lost their best dog that Saturday night. It got torn up badly and since they didn't dare take it to a vet, they shot it. That's what got to the woman who squealed on them. She could take the fighting, but not the needless killing."

A collective groan went up from the group.

"Their other dogs are in the training stage. One is only a pup, about three months old."

"It's not that dogs are mean. It's people who make them that way. But the dog gets blamed for anything that happens," Erica griped.

"Yeah, I know. We took those dogs down to the Humane Society shelter in Lincoln. If they aren't able to change their behavior, they'll be put down. Right now, those dogs would tear your arm off if you looked at them cross-eyed. They'll probably be able to do something with the pup, but I doubt if they can with the adult dogs."

"It's people who commit the crime, but the dogs that get killed for it. Its not fair!"

"I know its not. But what else could we do?"

"Stop the 'sport' of dog fighting in the first place."

"We're trying. Lincoln County will really go all out to shut down that place they were fighting. It was on a ranch not far from Lincoln."

"I hope they don't find another spot."

"Me too."

While the conversation ebbed and flowed, Clay leaned close to Erica and whispered in her ear, "I'd like to see you alone."

Erica got to her feet and said, "I've got to run down and check on a couple of animals." Clay got up and followed her.

At the foot of the stairs down to the basement clinic, he caught up with her.

"Hold up a minute."

She turned to face him, smiling. "Congratulations," she said. "You did it."

"Thanks to you." He reached out a long arm and propped himself in a leaning position against the wall. He gave her a mischievous grin. "I want to make an appointment to get my puppy vaccinated."

"Puppy? What are you going to do with a dog in that little room you live in?"

"I need one for my farm."

"Farm? Don't you already have several dogs out at the farm?"

"Not Dad's farm. Mine."

She stared at him. He looked down at her with his little-boy grin. "I'm going to take one of Herb's pups when they're old enough, the one with the most white on it. The father is a Border Collie."

"Or as Lena Lemm would say, a Borderline Collie. I understand the dog, but what's this about a farm?"

"I bought the Pettijohn place, lock stock and barrel, including the cow and calf."

Erica's mouth dropped open in amazement.

"I always thought I'd like to have a log cabin. There's only one thing missing."

"What? Let's see, you have a log cabin, a good barn, a woodlot that doubles as pasture, and a dog. Oh, you need a cat."

"I figure one will find its way out there one of these days."

"Then what?"

"I need someone to share it with."

There followed a long pause.

"Is this an invitation, a proposition or what?"

"Any way you'd like to take it?"

"Just what are you asking me?"

Clay looked down at the floor, shifted his weight off the wall and folded his arms. His tone became uncertain. "Maybe I'm asking too much. I kind of thought maybe you'd come and live with me. It's not as if we haven't — you know — done it before."

Erica sighed. She remembered that time all right; graduation night, a balmy night in early June, a clearing in the woods, an unashamed exploring of each other's bodies, and the discovery of the joys of sex. He'd been the only man she'd ever slept with, a memory she treasured. But Clay was asking for more than that.

"Clay, I'm not in a position to make a commitment like that right now."

"You don't have to marry me, just come live with me."

"I can't do that. I have Gram to think of."

"Do you mean you have to take care of her, or that she wouldn't approve of your 'living in sin'?"

"Part of each. But I need time to build up my practice. I'm not ready for another commitment right now."

"Oh, well. I'll have to wait a while. But Erica, come out and have dinner with me when I get moved in. I barbecue a mean steak!"

"All right, Clay, I'll take you up on that."

They both knew that neither would expect that evening to end with dinner. They sealed the bargain with a kiss.

The End

ORDER FORM

Order at:

Online:
www.DurangoPublishing.com
Telephone:
Toll free 1-800-545-6321 or 250-490-3000.
Have your credit card ready.
Email:
orders@DurangoPublishing.com
Mail:
Durango Publishing Corp.
Suite 204 - 69 Nanaimo Ave. E.
Penticton, BC, Canada V2A1M1

Dr. Erica Merrill Mystery Series: By Anne Barton
TILL HELL FREEZES OVER --$19.95 Cdn $16.95 US
A SWITCH IN TIME -- $15.95 Cdn $12.95 US

Add $4.95 shipping & handling, plus 7% GST if ordering from Canada. For each additional book shipped at the same time to the same address, S&H is only $2.95. S&H to the United States is $8.95 for the first book, and additional books to the same address are $5.95 each.

My check or money order is enclosed, or please charge my credit card: ☐Visa ☐MasterCard.
Payment must accompany orders.

Name _____

Address _____

City/Prov/PC _____

Phone _____ Email _____

Credit Card # _____

Expiration Date _____ Signature _____